# LINC⊛LNSHIRE COUNTY COUNCIL
## EDUCATION and CULTURAL SERVICES

**This book should be returned on or before the last date shown below.**

_QS/06_         MH2

2 3 SEP 2008

2 3 MAR 2009     1 8 JUL 2014

1 8 JUN 2012     - 9 FEB 2015

Quxo—

1 9 MAR 2013

C| Coleby

To renew or order library books visit
www.lincolnshire.gov.uk
You will require a Personal Identification Number.
Ask any member of staff for this

EC.199(LIBS):RS/L5/19

F FOLEY           16. OCT 03.

The girl who had everything.    07. NOV 03

£14.99            LARGE PRINT

L 5/9

# The Girl
## who had
# Everything

# The Girl
## who had
# Everything

RAE FOLEY

**Thorndike Press • Chivers Press**
**Thorndike, Maine USA  Bath, England**

This Large Print edition is published by Thorndike Press, USA and by Chivers Press, England.

Published in 1999 in the U.S. by arrangement with Golden West Literary Agency.

Published in 1999 in the U.K. by arrangement with Golden West Literary Agency.

U.S. Hardcover 0-7862-1879-7 (Candlelight Series Edition)
U.K. Hardcover 0-7540-3757-6 (Chivers Large Print)
U.K. Softcover  0-7540-3758-4 (Camden Large Print)

The text of this Large Print edition is unabridged.
Other aspects of the book may vary from the original edition.

Set in 16 pt. Plantin by Minnie B. Raven.

Printed in the United States on permanent paper.

**British Library Cataloguing in Publication Data available**

**Library of Congress Cataloging in Publication Data**

Foley, Rae, 1900–
    The girl who had everything / Rae Foley.
       p.  (large print)   cm.
    ISBN 0-7862-1879-7 (lg. print : hc : alk. paper)
    1. Large type books.  I. Title.
  [PS3511.O186G58   1999]
  813'.54—dc21                        99-11211

# The Girl
## who had
# Everything

# 1

The elopement of Mary Ann Rutherford with James Monk Bartlett crowded even the presidential campaign off the front page of the newspapers. Mary Ann was a phenomenon, a fabulously wealthy girl who was pretty, very pretty, and yet was regarded without envy or resentment — even with affection — by the public, which took an almost proprietary pride in her. She held in the public heart the kind of sentimental devotion that, a generation earlier, had been bestowed on Shirley Temple.

By the time she was seventeen the rumor mongers had already begun to speculate about a suitable marriage partner for her. There were some who even suggested royalty. Others were content to name a famous tennis player or a handsome actor or an aspiring young politician. Mary Ann moved quietly through all this publicity and speculation, with a charming smile, but also with a shade of aloofness that discouraged impertinent questions. She never allowed herself to be interviewed. When cornered, which was seldom, because she was as closely guarded as the child of a president, she simply shook her head, smiling but mute.

How much of this reticence was intrinsic and how much imposed was never suspected until after the tragedy. Then even the Rutherford power and influence could not silence the media altogether, and a picture began to emerge of the girl who, to protect her from kidnappers and other mischance, was always as securely locked away as though behind prison walls.

The wonder was that she could have broken free of that close supervision to elope. The greater wonder was that she ever encountered James Bartlett, because Jimmy did not move in the Rutherford circles. Actually he did not move in any circle. He had inherited a small antiques business, which he expanded to include an even smaller art collection, of mostly obscure artists, though occasionally Uncle Cliffe would make a real find on one of his endless trips abroad and send it on, usually with a casual letter saying that he had just happened to run across a rather nice little picture, probably valueless but pleasant. Uncle Cliffe hated to be thanked. Anyhow, I always suspected that he felt guilty, irrational as this was, because he had managed to make a lot of money and acquire a position of importance while his brother, like Jimmy, had been content to surround himself with beautiful things. He was regretful only when a determined customer insisted on buying something.

Like his father before him, Jimmy was totally unequipped to be a businessman. As a salesman he was just plain disastrous. When he found something he liked, he was reluctant to part with it and put it in the darkest, least accessible corner of the shop, hoping no one would notice it. And his bookkeeping was a nightmare.

That's why I took over the books and then, after Jimmy had primed me with the essential information, began to do the selling. Jimmy was my brother, four years older than I. After we had been orphaned and Uncle Cliffe had had to deputize someone to look after us, Jimmy voluntarily took on the responsibility of being a combination of parent, big brother, teacher, and watchdog for his little sister. I thought him the most wonderful person in the world, but I'd have taken a beating before I admitted it. Jimmy shied away from any display of sentimentality. In fact, he had a tendency to shy away from any personal relationship, which only compounded the mystery of his romantic elopement with America's darling.

As a present for my twenty-third birthday, Uncle Cliffe offered to take me along on one of his business trips, this time a six months' tour. His wife, who had always accompanied him, had been dead for four years. Uncle Cliffe talked little about his constant, far-reaching journeys, but we gathered that, heavily financed, he was searching the world over for all the basic sources of energy and, perhaps, ultimate destruction. Both Jimmy and I felt he had done so much for us as youngsters that we had no right to accept anything more, but this time Jimmy insisted that I go.

"Enjoy yourself for once without worrying about the shop, Jen. It won't fall apart in half a year. Maybe" — and he grinned — "you'll pick up an unknown Rembrandt and make our fortunes."

"Considering that the United States is rumored to possess ten times as many Rembrandts as the man ever painted, I wouldn't bank on it."

"And without some besotted male hanging around, taking your mind off your work and letting the business go to wrack and ruin, I might get some peace around here. Why don't you marry one of these guys and put him out of his misery? It would be an act of charity."

"It would be an act of insanity."

"What you need, Jen, is one of those strong, silent men — he'd have to be silent around you, anyhow — who'd show you what male dominance should be in a more perfect world."

"You're a fine one to talk."

"Just a mass of repressions, that's me. But one of these days I'm going to surprise you."

Which heaven knows he did when the news broke on a stunned world — and on me — that Mary Ann Rutherford had secretly married my brother.

## II

Three months later, when Uncle Cliffe and I had just returned to Western Europe from behind the Iron Curtain, laden down with all sorts of special permits and visas that gave him an entrée into what I had always assumed were closed circles, headlines hit the papers with all the force of an atomic bomb.

## MARY ANN RUTHERFORD SUICIDE

Bride of Three Months
Dead of Sleeping Pills

Three months after her secret marriage with James Monk Bartlett, owner of a small antiques business on Manhattan, Mary Ann Rutherford, heiress to one of America's great fortunes, lies dead from an overdose of sleeping pills. Her mother is in a state of collapse and cannot be interviewed. Her father, Paul Rutherford, industrialist, whose name has been mentioned as a candidate for a high post in the new administration, has issued a statement, declaring that if his daughter died by her own hand she was driven to it.

"This disastrous marriage," Mr. Rutherford declared, "was headed for trouble from the outset. How and where did Mary Ann encounter this shopkeeper? How did he persuade her to marry him within two weeks of their first meeting? I will find the answer to these questions if it takes the rest of my life."

James Bartlett had no comment to make. According to a close friend, he is stunned by the death of his young wife, to whom he was devoted, and he has no explanation as to why she should have wished to end her life.

Funeral services are to be private. Mr. Rutherford, who is in charge of the arrangements, asks that no flowers be sent but that contributions be made to increase protection for young girls from unscrupulous adventurers.

One television program showed a picture of the Rutherford estate on Long Island, the mansion's façade roughly the length of Buckingham Palace and with magnificent grounds behind a ten-foot fence. The grounds, the commentator said, were not only patrolled at night, but several savage dogs were allowed to roam free to discourage intruders. The commentator added brightly, "From this . . . to this." The picture shifted to the shabby little antiques shop on lower Madison, with an arrow indicating the apartment above it.

There were, inevitably, articles summing up the brief life of Mary Ann Rutherford, a life filled with public adulation, and yet "the girl who had everything" had voluntarily given it all up.

Or had she?

There were only two conclusions to be drawn from the devastating treatment of the story in the news media. Either Jimmy had driven his wife to take her life or he had killed her himself. Neither one was possible.

During the three months of the marriage,

while Uncle Cliffe and I were traveling through the Scandinavian countries, West Germany, and points east, we discussed every conceivable reason for that improbable marriage. I couldn't see Jimmy pursuing any girl, especially one of great wealth. It was not only that he was not interested in money; he had no profound interest in people. He was essentially a solitary person. The reason we had gotten along so well was that I had understood his need for solitude and hadn't tried to impinge on it. And Jimmy wasn't impulsive. The idea of his marrying, two weeks after meeting her, a girl accustomed to every conceivable luxury and taking her to that little apartment where she'd have to do her own housework didn't make sense.

"Perhaps not," Uncle Cliffe agreed with his usual amiability, "but the fact remains that it happened."

"How do you think it will work out?"

He shrugged. "One thing sticks out a mile. The girl was the aggressor. It's not in Jimmy's character. She has always had what she wanted. She went after him. When she gets tired of her bargain, she'll walk out."

"Poor Jimmy!"

Uncle Cliffe smiled at me. "Just because the two of you look alike doesn't mean that you are alike. You can't put yourself in his place. Want to bet that when or if she does leave him he'll be so deep in a book within a week he won't hear the bell when a customer walks in the shop?"

I had no answer to that, but I had a lot of questions. "Another thing, with all the possibilities — and that girl could have had anyone — why did she pick Jimmy? He has no money. He isn't the kind to sweep a girl off her feet. He doesn't create an electric atmosphere of excitement and gaiety around him. And all the Bartletts are cursed with red hair."

Uncle Cliffe, who is tall and broad and handsome, with touches of gray in his dark hair and enormous vigor — at fifty he could easily pass for forty — grinned at me.

"It missed me, and you are more auburn than red. Very becoming actually." From Uncle Cliffe, who doesn't flatter, that was equivalent to being compared with Nefertiti. "Of course, what gives you away is those green eyes and the silky black brows that tilt up at the corners. Satanic. People don't find either of you actually repulsive. In fact, I seem to remember a man named — what is it? — William something."

"Oh, that was months ago."

"And the current one? Don't try to tell me

15

you don't always have some poor misguided fellow dangling at your heels. Oh, yes, Philip Hanning is the latest victim."

"He's more Jimmy's friend than mine."

"Have it your own way," said Uncle Cliffe agreeably.

"I don't mean that I don't like Philip. I suppose he's the nicest man I've ever known — ever will know."

"Poor devil. That's a handicap few men could overcome."

But Uncle Cliffe let the matter drop there. He respected privacy. Since the death of his wife, whom he had dearly loved, he had never, so far as I knew, contemplated remarrying, though I was aware that occasionally there was a temporary interest in the background whom I never met. He was a wonderful companion, undemanding, always good-tempered, and full of delightful ideas. I'd never had such a wonderful time as during those months when Uncle Cliffe and I toured Europe, though I kept wondering and speculating, puzzled and disturbed. Jimmy's letters were brief and uninformative, but then he had never been one to feel any need to pour out his heart. My letter to Mary Ann, as warm and welcoming as I could make it, had remained unanswered.

One problem particularly concerned me. There would be no room for me in Jimmy's present household. I was pretty sure I could find a job if I decided not to marry Philip. But how was Jimmy going to run the shop without me? Somehow I couldn't see Mary Ann soft-talking a customer into buying some Paul Revere silver or the painting of an unknown artist.

But with the news of Mary Ann's suicide — or, as her father implied, murder — all this came to an end.

"I've got to go home," I said.

"We'll both go."

"But you shouldn't leave your job."

"Suppose," Uncle Cliffe said, "you let me worry about that. You pack and I'll arrange about airplane tickets."

"You mean right away?" I asked, surprised.

"Right away. In my opinion, time is of the essence."


### III


Actually, it was more than three weeks before we reached New York. That wasn't Uncle Cliffe's fault. Pressures were brought to bear by the big anonymous forces that actually rule our world, and he had to spend days making long-distance telephone calls, sending cables, writing reports, and talking with the groups he represented, who regarded family problems, however pressing, as trivial.

All I had to go on during the time we waited for release from Uncle Cliffe's duties was the news that came through in the papers and on the radio and television. Rutherford had attempted to bar his son-in-law from the funeral services, which Mrs. Rutherford, in a state of collapse, had been unable to attend. I saw pictures of the crowds in front of the funeral parlor — sightseers, photographers, reporters, and peeping Toms who come out from under stones. It was a disgusting exhibition. I couldn't find Jimmy anywhere in the crowd.

"Never mind, Jimmy; never mind," I kept repeating to myself, a meaningless and stupid incantation that meant nothing and achieved nothing.

In a way it was Uncle Cliffe who designed the shape of things to come. Before we landed at Kennedy Airport he turned for a critical look at me as I was hastily powdering my nose and slipping into the fur coat he had given me. It would have been mink if I hadn't balked. "I thought mink was reserved for paying off kept women," I'd said.

So Uncle Cliffe had laughed and gotten me a dyed muskrat, which was beautiful, warm, and suited me to a T.

He drew from his pocket a pair of dark glasses, huge ones that seemed to cover half my face.

"But I never wear dark glasses!"

"Anyone who has ever seen Jimmy would recognize you as his sister by those eyes and tilted brows. People notice them, and we want to avoid being noticed, don't we?"

Wordlessly I slipped on the glasses, aware of a chill. I stole a look at Uncle Cliffe, but there was no reading that impassive face. I wondered what he had been learning from various unofficial sources during those past weeks. No one noticed us as we made our way out to collect our luggage, and Uncle Cliffe deftly snared a taxicab from under the nose of an energetic man who had been waving his arms like a semaphore.

Because he was in New York only for brief intervals, Uncle Cliffe did not maintain an apartment, but he kept a year-round suite at the Plaza, high up and with a view the length of Central Park. He had taken it because Lady Mary had loved the view, though he never referred to that. Their marriage had had a completeness that was a rare and precious thing.

I remembered her as a rather tall woman, though she must have been still a girl when I knew her and visited at Glydes Park. But she had seemed old to me then, as all grown-ups did. She was fair, with a marvelous complexion, a superb horsewoman, and good at most sports. Uncle Cliffe once said that the Glydes stables were among the finest in England and about the last thing to be sold when her father, the marquis, could no longer maintain the expense of a great estate. He had talked things over with his son and heir, who had readily agreed that the place would have to be sold in spite of having been in the family for three hundred years. It had been bought by an Arab oil man, but Lady Mary's brother simply shrugged and refused to discuss it. *"Autres temps, autres moeurs,"* he said. Like his sister, he wasn't one to whimper.

He had refused financial assistance from Uncle Cliffe, though they remained the best of friends, and I had come to know him well on his frequent trips to the United States, where, at Uncle Cliffe's insistence, he put up at the Plaza suite.

In adversity the Glydes maintained an outward dignity and a complete lack of self-pity, which brought me back — though I was never far from it — to the mystery of Mary

Ann, who had rejected life so inexplicably.

When the taxi pulled up at the little antiques shop, Uncle Cliffe gave a sharp exclamation. Then he said, "Wait here, Jennifer." There was one big window, beautifully adapted for displays, but it had been boarded up and slivers of glass glittered on the sidewalk.

I climbed out of the taxi and ran to join Uncle Cliffe, who, after trying the door, was ringing the bell, a two-toned affair. The shop door was locked, although it was nearly eleven o'clock.

A patrolman strolled up behind us. "Move on," he said.

"My brother lives here. What happened?"

"Someone smashed the windows last night and got away with some stuff."

"Oh, burglars," Uncle Cliffe said, and there was relief his voice. But what had he expected? "Know who did this?"

"It was reported about four this morning, and the worst of the glass has been cleared up. The owner" — and then he snapped to attention — "Mr. Bartlett, the one who —" The patrolman broke off, staring at me.

"Is he all right?" I asked.

"I wouldn't know. I tried to talk to him this morning. He just looked at me, dazed, and then when I asked him what was missing he pulled himself together and made a list. Never even thought of having the window boarded up or calling the insurance people until I told him. He didn't seem to be all there."

The door opened on a chain. "Not open for business today."

"Jimmy! It's Jen. Jen and Uncle Cliffe."

The door opened then. Jimmy had aged in the months since I had seen him. This morning he had not troubled to shave. He looked as though he hadn't slept for a week. He wore wrinkled dark slacks and a snagged pullover with a hole in one elbow. He stood staring at us, swaying a little. At first I thought he was drunk, though Jimmy practically never drank hard liquor. He did pride himself, however, on being something of a connoisseur of fine wines. Once I had pointed out that gin and vodka cost less, but he hadn't bothered to reply except by an expressive shudder.

As usual it was Uncle Cliffe who took charge. He said, "When did you last eat anything?"

Jimmy looked at him vaguely and shook his head.

"He's in shock." Uncle Cliffe glanced toward the boarded-up window. "Any violence?"

"Queer thing," the patrolman put in, "there must have been a hell of a racket when that window was smashed. The man on patrol found some guy coming home from a big night who told him he'd heard the crash and seen a truck outside the shop and a couple of guys carrying out a piece of furniture."

"He didn't try to stop them?"

The patrolman laughed cynically. "You think this is Utopia or something? He said he was one against two, and anyhow they were probably armed and he was the worse for wear."

"He didn't even report it?"

"He didn't want to get mixed up in anything. What about this guy Bartlett? Is he drunk or nuts?"

"He's in shock," Uncle Cliffe repeated patiently. He turned to me. "Get him upstairs and then rustle up some food. I'll take care of the luggage and the taxi."

The patrolman observed the competent way Uncle Cliffe was handling things and, after a moment's hesitation, he strolled on. Uncle Cliffe never throws his weight around, but no one can miss his unstressed authority.

Jimmy, with uncharacteristic meekness, let me steer him up to the small living room we had shared for five years. But it wasn't meekness, I realized; just apathy. I pushed him into a chair beside the fireplace and, realizing that he was chilled, I lighted a presto log, and went into the little kitchen to get him some food. The place was dirty; there were soiled dishes in the sink and practically nothing in the refrigerator or on the shelves, except for the basic supplies I always kept on hand. The whole apartment had a dingy, neglected air about it.

There was a delicatessen around the corner, as there is almost everywhere in New York, and I brushed past Uncle Cliffe, who was paying off the cabbie, and explained that I was going out to get some food.

The man at the delicatessen did not recognize me, though I had been shopping there for years, so apparently the dark glasses were effective, as was the new fur coat. I was relieved in a way, because I was in no mood for talk — not the kind I was bound to hear after Mary Ann's suicide and the break-in of the shop, which, of course, would be common knowledge to the whole neighborhood by now.

When I came back with two heavy bags of groceries, I found Uncle Cliffe relaxed and meditative in his chair. He sat facing Jimmy, who was sprawled out, arms dangling limply, fingers trailing on the thin carpet, eyes half closed. There was something defenseless, vulnerable in his tired face. I wanted to cry out, "What has she done to you?" but Uncle Cliffe, who knows me rather well, made a faint gesture and I went out to the kitchen and prepared coffee, toast, and scrambled eggs.

I put the tray on Jimmy's lap. "You eat every scrap of that."

I think it was the first time that he was really aware of my presence. He straightened up with a jerk that nearly upset the coffee and started to push the tray away. I pushed it back. He smiled then, and Jimmy has the most delightful smile. I was about to make some infuriated comment on the way he had been neglecting himself when Uncle Cliffe forestalled me.

"What happened down there?"

Jimmy took a swallow of coffee, tasted the eggs, and then began to eat hungrily. I looked on in satisfaction. No one spoke until he had finished every scrap, and then he sat back, shaking his head a bit as though to clear it. The green eyes were sparkling now like the ocean with the sun on it, and they had lost that frightening cloudiness.

"Just part of the pattern," he said, going

back to Uncle Cliffe's question.

"Lose much?"

"That Queen Carlotta dressing table. Finest association piece I had and in perfect condition, the provenance clear all the way."

"Did you call the insurance people?" I asked.

When Jimmy made no answer I repeated my question.

"There's been a bit of trouble about that."

"What kind of trouble?"

"They want to cancel my insurance."

"Why?"

"It looks," Jimmy said, "as though someone is trying to destroy the business." He added, "And me."

# 2

"Who?" I asked.

"Who?" Uncle Cliffe asked.

"Rutherford, of course," Jimmy said almost casually. "He's been breathing fire ever since Mary Ann — he blames me, you know. And he is going to wreck me."

"Aren't you a bit overwrought?" Uncle Cliffe said in his usual tranquil tone.

"Oh, he's proclaimed it far and wide."

I noticed that Uncle Cliffe was observing him sharply. "Somehow," he drawled, "I can't see a man of Rutherford's type smashing a store window and making off with a — whatever it was."

"He'd use hired goons for that, of course. He's been quite the busy little bee. The day after Mary Ann's funeral — and, by the way, a couple of his strongmen prevented me from attending the services — a man came in and bought the little Sisley, the one you sent me last year, Uncle Cliffe, and the biggest single sale I've ever made. Next day all hell broke loose. The buyer called and said an expert declared it was a fake. Then he

27

came along with his expert, a lawyer, and the — at least *a* painting. And the damned thing was a copy. A put-up job if there ever was one. I wasn't going to give back that money. I'd sold a genuine Sisley, and they had the thing in their possession. I called my lawyer, who said he couldn't handle the case for me. Going out of private practice. So Rutherford had got to him as he had to the insurance people.

"Two days later my pickup truck for delivering furniture had all four tires slashed. Day before yesterday there was an article in the *Chronicle* warning people about dishonest art dealers. On the heels of the publicity over the fake Sisley, you can imagine the pointing fingers I got. And last night my display window was smashed and the dressing table was stolen."

Jimmy accepted a cigarette and light from Uncle Cliffe and leaned back in his chair. I saw then the depth of his exhaustion.

"How sure are you that Rutherford is behind this campaign — if it is a campaign?"

"One hundred percent. He doesn't want just to ruin the business. He wants me dead."

Uncle Cliffe started to say something, changed his mind, went downstairs. I heard the front door close. After a while I stretched out my hand and Jimmy took it, let it go, and his own dropped limply on the carpet again.

At last I said, "Jimmy, how on earth did you ever meet Mary Ann? With her background the chances of you even seeing her face to face —"

"It was the damnedest thing. We met in an elevator."

"An elevator!"

He nodded, an odd smile flickering around his mouth. "I'd been to see my dentist and got in this self-service elevator, and the girl darted in after me as though she was running away from someone and jabbed the bell. Well, I knew who she was at first glance, of course. Mary Ann Rutherford. Much prettier even than her pictures, because her coloring was so lovely. I hadn't realized that she had brown eyes with that bright gold hair. They were something.

"Well, all of a sudden, the elevator stopped between floors. We didn't know it then, of course, but that was the time when — oh, you were abroad and wouldn't remember. All the power in midtown Manhattan was off for a couple of hours. So there we were. I didn't speak because, from what I'd heard, I expected to be frostbitten, but she began to talk. She wasn't scared about the power being off. I think she enjoyed it. In fact, I know she did. By the end of an hour we were sitting on the floor and gabbing away as though we were old friends. I'd figured her as being sophisticated as hell, but she was just a kid, a twelve-year-old kid playing hooky. But for all that she seemed so surprisingly young for her age, she packed a real charge. Any man would have felt it half a block away, and in an elevator . . .

" 'Don't ever let anyone tell you it's fun to have a lot of money, Jimmy,' she said. 'You're never free to be yourself. If I hadn't just leaped into this elevator, I'd have my private bodyguard right with me and, believe me, you and I would not be talking to each other. And one thing sure, she'll be waiting whenever this thing gets going again. I wish it would never move.' "

"She called you Jimmy right away?"

"Right away." There was a touch of grimness in my brother's voice but, to my relief, he did not seem to mind talking about his tragically dead young bride. In a way, I think he was relieved to talk the thing out.

"Well, she asked what I did and whether I was married and all sorts of stuff. She —"
For the first time his voice broke. "You've

30

The handwriting was unformed, almost a child's writing:

I'm sorry, Jimmy. I hoped it would work. I guess you did your best, but you couldn't help being poor. I can't go home and I can't go on like this.

I know it's just like going to sleep, so I shouldn't be afraid. I wish I didn't keep remembering that Shakespeare thing you read to me:

Ay, but to die and go we know not where,
To lie in cold obstruction and to rot . . .

Ugh! Well, good night, Jimmy. I wonder where I'll be saying good morning. Mary Ann.


## II


"My candid opinion," Uncle Cliffe said in a tone I'd never heard him use before, "is that your late wife was a bitch, Jimmy. You are well out of it."

"Oh, no," Jimmy said, "she was just a kid — literally. And scared. She hated living like this, but she didn't know how to handle it.

35

She'd never had to handle anything in her life, you see, so she took the easy way out."

"But why?" I asked. "Surely it wasn't just because she couldn't cook or look after the apartment."

"No," Jimmy said heavily. "It was something she did not know how to handle in any other way. You see, I was given a copy of the autopsy report, just as Rutherford was. Mary Ann was four months pregnant when she died, and how Rutherford managed to keep that out of the papers God only knows. It wasn't my kid, Jen. I swear to that. But Rutherford thinks it was. He thinks I tricked her into marriage. He thinks — heaven knows what he thinks! But he is going to smash me. So I want you to clear out of this. Get right away and stay away. Finish that tour with Uncle Cliffe. You might not be safe here with me."

"If you think for one minute," I sputtered, "that I'm going to walk out on you at a time like this, you're out of your cotton-pickin' mind. I'll see Mr. Rutherford myself. I'll tell him —"

Uncle Cliffe broke in with his usual calm. "If I might interject a word of common sense into this melodrama," he said, and for the first time Jimmy and I laughed at each other in our old way. "There are moments,"

Uncle Cliffe went on, "when I despair of either of you ever achieving any capacity for logical thought. What leaps to my mind is Rutherford's overreaction to the whole situation. On the face of it, his determination to isolate Mary Ann from the world is absurd. Even a president's children are allowed a reasonably long leash. What was Rutherford really afraid of?"

"Afraid?" Obviously Jimmy was trying to absorb a new idea.

Uncle Cliffe took time to light a cigar. "How well did you know your mother-in-law?" he asked unexpectedly.

"I never saw her. After Rutherford barged in here breathing fire I never saw or heard of Mary Ann's family and I don't think she did either."

"Did she seem to mind?"

"She hardly ever mentioned her parents. She resented her father, naturally. I don't know how she felt about her mother."

"No grieving over having caused her any unhappiness?"

"Oh, no."

"And Mrs. Rutherford never tried to get in touch with her only child."

"Not as far as I know."

"Who" — Uncle Cliffe went off on another tangent — "was Mary Ann's physician?"

"She didn't have one. She hated doctors."

"But, good lord, there must have been a doctor, Jimmy. The girl must have known she was pregnant. She'd be bound to consult someone."

"I tell you she hated doctors. She was afraid of them, terrified of them."

"But, my dear boy, someone provided those sleeping pills."

Jimmy shrugged.

For a while Uncle Cliffe smoked in silence, watching the little blue flame that ran around the end of the log.

I was forced to break through the quiet, which was getting on my nerves, it was so troubled. "I'll bet that if I could get in touch with Mrs. Rutherford I could make her see reason. I could arrange to have her meet Jimmy. She couldn't help believing in him then, could she? And then she could call off the dogs."

"In the first place," Uncle Cliffe said, "you'd never in the world be able to get in touch with Mrs. Rutherford. On Long Island she lives behind an electrified fence. In that Fifth Avenue apartment there are servants and guards and God knows what between her and people to reach her for one reason or another, chiefly to get money out of her, of course. And as Jimmy's sister —"

"But," I said in excitement, "they needn't know I am Jimmy's sister. With those dark glasses that cover my eyes, no one would notice the resemblance, and, anyhow, Mrs. Rutherford has never seen Jimmy."

"I find that very interesting," Uncle Cliffe said. "I've been seeking in vain for a plausible explanation of a mother wiping out her only child in this fashion. The chances are, Jennifer, that Mrs. Rutherford has no deep concern either about her daughter or her daughter's husband."

"In any case," Jimmy said, aroused momentarily out of his apathy, "I won't have it. I'm not going to let Rutherford get his filthy paws on Jen. I tell you the man is capable of anything. Oh, I don't mean anything melodramatic like murder, but smearing her reputation as he is smearing mine — things she can't fight."

"I can too fight."

"What I fail to understand," Uncle Cliffe said, "is this campaign of Rutherford's against Jimmy. I still claim the man is afraid, but what is he afraid of?" He was obviously thinking aloud and not expecting an answer, so Jimmy and I waited. "All this super-protection of Mary Ann isn't natural. Why was the girl kept on such a short leash?"

Jimmy started to speak and then his lips set tightly.

Uncle Cliffe was quick to understand. "No, I don't mean her pregnancy. Given the circumstances, it was almost inevitable that at the first opportunity she would be off in search of a little freedom, a life of her own. But why wasn't she allowed any?"

"I told you she was just a kid," Jimmy said tiredly.

"Twenty, wasn't she?"

"Well — oh, hell, what difference does it make now? Mary Ann was — not retarded actually — but she hadn't developed mentally much beyond the twelve-year-old level. Physically she had grown up. Someone had taught her a lot of surprising things." Jimmy broke off, and then he said in a tone I'd never heard him use in his life, "Taking advantage of a child, debauching her. That's one guy I'd like to get my hands on."

"Did you love her very much?" I asked bluntly.

Jimmy did not seem to resent this attempt to invade his private life. "I was knocked off my feet at first. Her looks, her sweetness, her helplessness, a childlike quality, and — Oh, what's the use? It's unspeakable to talk of her like this. Actually when I got over being besotted and we had long evenings together,

I realized we had nothing to talk about." He laughed suddenly. "Can you imagine what a fool I was? Trying to read Shakespeare to her? It didn't take long to discover that I had set up a child as a life companion — a corrupted child. The whole thing was a nightmare."

Uncle Cliffe and I sat stricken. Jimmy looked from one to the other and then he laughed harshly. "Good God! I didn't want to hurt her. I just wanted to protect her. I'm sorry as hell she solved her problem the way she did, but I can't help feeling there was no future for her. She would always need someone to protect her from other people as well as from herself. I can understand Rutherford's reason for having someone take care of her, but I think he went at it the wrong way. Still, I didn't do much better, did I?"

Uncle Cliffe refilled our glasses. "There's nothing we can do now about Mary Ann, but let's consider this man Rutherford. He's built what appears to be a fabulous fortune in a little over twenty-five years. Interlocking companies so interlocked I suppose not even the Treasury boys could sort them out. Power all over the place. Wherever I go I hear rumors, unsubstantiated and unsavory, regarding his business methods and his

41

holdings. He appears to be a bad enemy and nobody's friend but his own. There are as many stories circulating about him as there were about Howard Hughes, that ghastly warning to anyone who wants to pile money on money and power on power."

"What makes a man like that so greedy?" I asked.

"God knows. Right now, if rumor is to be relied on, Rutherford is working behind the scenes with the new administration. He'd like to be the puppet master, I suppose, but somewhere there's a weak link, something he wants concealed, and I'd be willing to wager that Mary Ann knew what it was. And that, my boy, is why Rutherford is out to discredit you. He is scared as hell that she told you."

"She didn't," Jimmy said. "But this other guy, the baby's father, might have known."

"I'd give something to get into that ménage," Uncle Cliffe said. "Introductions are easy enough, but nobody gets really close to Rutherford without being screened. The fact that I am a Bartlett and you are my nephew wouldn't take long to emerge."

"I can do it," I said.

"No!" Jimmy exclaimed.

"And, what's more, I am going to do it."

"You," Jimmy told me bluntly, "are a damned fool."

"Let's talk this over," Uncle Cliffe suggested. "It's obvious that something has to be done."

"And what," Jimmy asked, "will Philip have to say about this? He's been haunting the apartment ever since Mary Ann died, though he sort of steered clear while we were married. He is going to put his foot down."

"I can manage Philip," I said loftily.

"Don't overreach yourself, Jen. Did you ever get a look at that guy's jaw? He's not like the other men who hang around you, putty in your hands."

"Leave Philip to me," I said.

Someone ran lightly up the stairs. "Now," Philip said, "that's just what I want to hear." He grinned at Jimmy, waved cheerfully at Uncle Cliffe, and lifted me out of my chair to plant a kiss somewhat inaccurately on my nose. "Shall we set the date now?"

"You," I told him coldly, "have wandered into the wrong script."

Uncle Cliffe poured a glass of sherry and handed it to Philip. "Since my graceless niece and nephew have no manners, let me play host in this dismal establishment."

He and Philip had taken to each other from the start. Philip is nice looking but not too smooth, he has good manners that are not overstressed, he is athletic without flexing his muscles, he is prospering in the brokerage business without making a song and dance about it.

Philip Hanning had wandered into the shop about nine months earlier, attracted by a Chinese chess set in the window. He and Jimmy had started to talk about chess and had ended up in the apartment arguing about whether Bartok was possible on the harpsichord. Before he left I sold him the Chinese set for an outrageous price, and he had been coming back ever since. After the first few times he gave up the pretense of being a customer.

Now I saw him take a swift, cautious look at Jimmy. Apparently he was relieved to find him relaxed and smiling. I wondered how much he had known or guessed about that ill-fated marriage, but one thing I could bank on. He had never discussed it with Jimmy, and he never would without Jimmy's encouragement. Philip was, as I have said, a nice man, just about the nicest I knew.

"And now," he said when he had finished the sherry, "why am I to be left in your grubby paws, Jennifer? Never did I think . . ."

So I told him the whole thing. When I had finished he glanced at Jimmy. "Old Stone

44

Face. So you've been keeping all this to yourself. But you can hardly hide that boarded-up window, can you? And there's a lawyer and an insurance company who need some investigation. You know, I don't like this."

Jimmy laughed outright but Philip went on soberly, "I don't like any part of it, but Jennifer is right. It can't go on. A man like Rutherford must not be allowed to operate as he pleases. All I wish is that Jennifer could be kept out of it."

"She'll be kept out," Jimmy said.

"She can't be," Philip told him gently. "So far as I can see, Jennifer is the only one who can bore her way into that stronghold and find out what gives, and this is going to take a little planning."

Jimmy scoffed but Uncle Cliffe said, "Go on. We're listening."

Philip held out his glass for a refill. Then he began to talk. He talked for a long time.

# 3

The first part of the plan was for me to move out of the apartment I had shared with Jimmy, in case anyone should check up on me. Philip found me a reasonably comfortable furnished room in the West Eighties and I moved in without delay.

We had argued hotly about the name I would take. If it was true that anyone who came within shooting distance of a Rutherford was thoroughly screened, nothing could be left to chance. I must have a background I knew thoroughly and over which I would not be likely to trip, as I am the world's most unconvincing liar.

In the class ahead of me in high school there had been a girl named Mary Ann Weldone, whom I remembered vaguely as negative to the point of invisibility. She lived with a widowed mother who did dressmaking and who died just before Mary Ann graduated from high school.

She had talked to me about her plans chiefly because there wasn't anyone else for her to talk to. She didn't make friends easily.

46

The chances were that she had long since vanished into the turbulence of Manhattan like a drop of water in a rainstorm. She had no skills, and employment possibilities had always been severely limited, as she lacked both imagination and initiative.

It was the name Mary Ann that aroused most of the controversy, though from the beginning Jimmy steadily set himself against the whole plan. Philip agreed that here was an ideal personality for me to adopt. I knew the school, I knew the background, I knew the names of a number of the teachers and the pupils, and it was highly unlikely that anyone would find any trace of Mary Ann. But that name was the joker in the pack. The Rutherfords would sheer away from anyone with that name and be suspicious from the start.

"Or it could be my ace in the hole," I said. "Anyhow, I have a hunch . . ." Both Philip and Jimmy groaned.

Before moving to my new address under my new name I thought of something we had all passed over as of no importance. "Look, it is five years since I last saw Mary Ann. There's got to be some record of those years that can be checked on."

Remembering the poor girl's lack of training, we tried to figure out any way she could have found of earning her living.

"She was a door mat," I said. "The kind that people just automatically take advantage of, the kind to be a self-effacing slave to some tiresome old woman."

"That's an idea," Philip said, "a companion. Privately employed. That takes care of a lot of problems. Now we've got to make it seem as though you have been looking for a job."

So I put an ad in *The New York Times*, applying for a job as a companion, and Philip prepared two letters of introduction for me. One of them, written by Philip himself, said I had been a valued and cheerful companion for his aunt until her death two years before. I had a way of building up her depressed spirits, and I was highly reliable. She had even turned over to me the payment of her bills, balancing her checkbook, making out her income tax.

The second letter was prepared as a joke by a woman friend of Philip's — "Before I met you," he assured me hastily, ignoring Jimmy's wide grin — who wrote that she found me a delightful companion and would never have parted with me if she had not decided to move to Switzerland to live with some retired friends.

"Just retiring their money," Philip explained. "No taxes."

So I moved into the furnished room, still over Jimmy's protests, and arranged to communicate through a post office box number on the assumption that Jimmy's telephones in apartment and shop might be tapped. If at any time three days were to pass without word from me, he would know I was in trouble.

"There are times," Uncle Cliffe remarked, "when I suspect you see yourself as a female James Bond." That was the last time we saw him, as he yielded to *force majeure* and returned to Europe. "At least," he said, "Bert flew in last night from England, and he'll be at the Plaza if you need him. He is fascinated and says you can call on him for anything short of murder." Bert was his brother-in-law, the present Marquis of Glydes.

## II

In the next couple of weeks I got only three responses to my ad applying for a position as companion for an elderly woman. One was for house-to-house canvassing. One wanted a healthy young girl who would prefer a good home to salary and would help with the housework and cooking and look after three small children. No money was mentioned. A good home, apparently, was above rubies. The third was from a bachelor who wanted a young female assistant to work with him on a book in a "retired spot." At least the poor dope who fell for that one couldn't say she hadn't been warned. The man might be a snake, but at least he rattled before he struck.

Those two weeks dragged unbearably, but I didn't dare try to hasten things. I still had no plan at all. Somehow or other I hoped to get into the Rutherford household, and having to mark time was maddening. But at least there was an apparent respite in hostilities and nothing more had happened to Jimmy, though he admitted that business had fallen off disastrously because of the publicity about the fake Sisley.

Every day I mailed a card to the post office box, and then, wearing the huge dark glasses, I began, as cautiously as I could, to keep an eye on the Rutherford establishment.

All those big Fifth Avenue apartment buildings have doormen, of course, and when I passed the Rutherford building I chose a time of day when there were a number of people on the sidewalk, so I wouldn't be noticed. Inside the door I could see what looked like an armed guard.

One thing I didn't dare risk was loitering. I'd be spotted at once. But one day when I was walking on the Central Park side of the street I saw a girl who sat on a bench, coat collar turned up around her ears, shivering.

"You'll have to go farther down to get a bus," I told her.

"Thanks, I'm just waiting." She grinned at me. She had a nice, plain face with freckles and, at the moment, a red nose. "I'm not crazy; I'm just trying to earn a bonus."

"By showing how long you can sit here without freezing?"

"Oh, that would be simple compared with this assignment. I get two hundred and fifty smackers if I can pull off an interview with Mrs. Paul Rutherford. This is the fourth day I've waited for a glimpse of her. If I don't make it in one more day, I'll give up."

"What is she like?"

"That," the girl admitted, "is the sixty-four-thousand-dollar question. She is never photographed except for occasional group pictures, attending charity matinées and that sort of thing — the stuff that appears in society pages, not in the news. Right now she is said to be in a state of collapse as a result of her daughter's suicide, if it was a suicide. Well, what I really mind is having Pete beat me to it."

"Who is Pete?"

"Photographer on another paper. He's after a bonus, too."

"How do you expect to recognize Mrs. Rutherford if you've never seen even a good picture of her?"

"There's a big Lincoln with a dreamboat of a chauffeur that parks right in front of this bench, across the street from the apartment building, in case she wants to go out, which she doesn't seem to do. I don't blame the poor woman for breaking down, with her only child dying like that. Terrible! I guess the whole country has mourned for Mary Ann. And as for the guy who drove her to it — if that is all he did . . ."

I took a long breath and counted slowly, repeating to myself, "Don't lose your temper; don't lose your temper."

"Well, my comfort is that he'll get his," the girl said. "That will be a real satisfaction. I don't usually believe in an eye for an eye, but this is different. Personally I'd rather have a guard dog after me than that man Rutherford, if half what they say in the city room is true. I suppose this Bartlett man was after the poor kid's money. A sweet chance he has of collecting!" She began to sneeze and got up. "I can't take any more today."

I watched her walk down Fifth Avenue and turn the corner going east. My first eagerness for action had begun to fade, but after listening to her my resolve hardened. Whatever happened, someone had to protect Jimmy and stop Rutherford from attempting to destroy him. That was the first time I found myself considering seriously Uncle Cliffe's theory that Rutherford's ruthless vindictiveness toward Jimmy was a result of fear that Jimmy knew something damaging against him.

Next day I walked slowly along the park, looking at the entrance to the apartment house. There was a brisk breeze and the doorman was content to stay in the shelter of the lobby. A Lincoln purred up beside me and stopped; the driver slid out from under the wheel and stood waiting. So this was it. In a few minutes the door of the building opened and a woman came out, wearing a sable coat and hat and accompanied by a woman in a black coat. I remembered Jimmy's description of Mary Ann's companion: tall, thin, with a face like the side of a flatiron. She took Mrs. Rutherford's arm and tried to lead her across the street. The chauffeur stood at attention, but the woman in the sable coat shook her head, pulled her arm free, and started walking south down Fifth Avenue.

Her companion spoke to her, expostulating, indicating the waiting car. Stubbornly the woman kept on walking and, after a despairing look at the chauffeur and a shrug of the shoulders, the companion accompanied her. The chauffeur slammed the door of the Lincoln, put the car in gear, and then crawled slowly along the avenue in the direction the women had taken.

At the corner I waited for lights, crossed the avenue, and followed them. Mrs. Rutherford, now that she had had her own way, was chatting amiably to her companion. This kind of trailing was almost too easy, and I drifted in the wake of the two women, careful not to get too close.

The thing happened at Tiffany's, which, of course, was the really dangerous spot because unknown customers are closely watched in great jewelry shops. Obviously Mrs. Rutherford was well known there, judging by the way she was greeted.

"What can we show you today?" the clerk asked.

"I want to get a bracelet for my daughter's birthday," Mrs. Rutherford said, and my blood ran cold. "A diamond bracelet."

As the story of Mary Ann's suicide had

been highlighted in press and radio and television, the clerk could not prevent a startled look. Then he was graven-faced, noncommittal.

"Of course, madam."

"This is foolish of you, Mrs. Rutherford," the companion said. "You must try to face reality, as your husband told you. Your daughter is dead."

"She can't be dead. She can't. That's a wicked lie. She'll be home in a few days. She is just visiting friends."

The clerk, a polite smile plastered on his mouth, got out a tray of diamond bracelets and waited expressionlessly. Mrs. Rutherford bent over the tray, picking up one bracelet after another.

"Really, Mrs. Rutherford," her companion protested, "this is absurd."

The woman's insistence was as stupid as it was useless. It merely redoubled Mrs. Rutherford's resistance, which the companion would have realized if she had had a lick of common sense. I found myself unexpectedly a fierce partisan of the beleaguered woman, though the last thing I had anticipated was having any sympathy for a Rutherford.

She turned at bay. "I've had enough. This is intolerable. I want you to leave me at once. Go back to the apartment and ask my secretary to give you a check for three months' salary. Now go. I don't want to hear another word."

"You are dismissing me?"

"Definitely."

"What will Mr. Rutherford say?"

There was a flicker of alarm on Mrs. Rutherford's face, and I wondered whether she was afraid of her husband. Was she as carefully shut away from the world as her daughter had been? But her voice was firm.

"You heard me."

The woman turned and went out of the store, spots of rage burning on her cheeks. Mrs. Rutherford gave a little sigh of relief and half smiled. She bent over the tray again and selected a bracelet.

"Now that Mary Ann is older it will be all right for her to wear something like this. Will you charge it, please? I'll take it with me."

At the same moment I saw, out of the corner of my eye, the young man who was hovering near me, heard the click, and saw the tiny camera. There was no foresight in it, simply impulse. I grabbed the camera, dropped it, ground it under my foot.

"Hey," he expostulated, "what do you think you're doing?"

"Of all the filthy tricks," I said furiously. "Invading privacy."

"Also earning my living. The story of that bracelet for a dead daughter is no good without the picture." He picked up the battered camera, practically keening over it.

By this time people had gathered around us: Mrs. Rutherford, startled and wary; the photographer, angry as an enraged bull; the harassed clerk and me.

"What is it?" Mrs. Rutherford asked.

"He took a picture of you buying the bracelet. He sneaked up and took a picture."

For a moment Mrs. Rutherford was shaken. "My husband won't like that at all. He does not care to have publicity about me in the press." She turned to the clerk. "I think this young man had better be asked to leave, don't you?"

Without apparent fuss the photographer was hustled out of the shop, though I heard him protesting bitterly when he was outside, waving his broken camera like a talisman.

The clerk handed Mrs. Rutherford her package, a jewel box exquisitely wrapped, and turned to me inquiringly. I shook my head. "I just wanted to see what Tiffany's was like. I couldn't possibly afford to buy anything here."

Mrs. Rutherford smiled at me. "Thank you, my dear. That was very kind."

"Well, it was such a beastly thing to do! I just got mad." Then I gulped. "Golly, I suppose I'll have to pay for his camera."

"Don't worry. If the question arises, refer him to me. I am most grateful to you. What is your name?"

I swallowed and my throat and lips felt dry. "Mary Ann Weldone."

The pupils of her eyes dilated. "Mary Ann," she said in a tone of wonder. "Mary Ann. It's like a token." She put her hand on my arm and spoke almost pleadingly. "Won't you come home and have tea with me?"

The clerk had put away the tray of bracelets, but he was listening avidly and I saw the swift sardonic glance he cast in my direction.

"Well, I — well, you don't really owe me anything, you know."

"Do come." At the first indication of resistance she became insistent. She intended to have her own way. Perhaps her victory over her companion had given her new confidence in herself. It occurred to me that this wealthy woman, one of the pampered of the earth as one would suppose, rarely managed to see her own wishes fulfilled.

"Thank you very much," I said.

# III

I got my first taste of the relentless Rutherford surveillance when we were bowed out onto Fifth Avenue by the bland clerk who had waited on Mrs. Rutherford. Outside the door stood one of the best-looking men I'd ever seen. That was the first thing I noticed, the first thing any woman would notice. The second thing was that he wore a chauffeur's uniform and a cap over sleek black hair.

"The car is waiting, madam." He gave me a swift look, puzzled to know where I had come from. Mrs. Rutherford sighed and then passively let him escort her across the street and into the luxurious warmth of the car.

"Home?" he asked.

"Yes, home." She leaned back and shut her eyes. Now, at close range I could see how ravaged her face was. There were dark smudges under her eyes and her mouth twitched.

The car moved noiselessly down Fifth Avenue, turned east to Madison, and shortly turned again over to Fifth Avenue. Once more the chauffeur escorted us across the street. I had the curious sensation of being herded by a sheep dog. I wondered why the all-powerful Rutherford hadn't succeeded in suspending the one-way traffic law on Fifth Avenue for his personal convenience.

The doorman took a quick, shrewd look at me. Inside, the man who seemed to be an armed guard stepped forward and then, as Mrs. Rutherford swept past toward the elevators, he moved toward the house telephone.

When the elevator came to a halt on the twelfth floor, the door opened and a trim maid admitted us.

"We'll have tea in my sitting room," Mrs. Rutherford said and led the way through the foyer and a fantastic drawing room with floor-length windows opening on Central Park, up an enchanting circular staircase, and along a corridor into a small sitting room where another maid was waiting to take our coats.

When she had gone Mrs. Rutherford said abruptly, "Mary Ann. That's my daughter's name, you know."

She's mad as a March hare, I thought, in a kind of horror, yet with a dreadful kind of pity, too.

An overweight middle-aged woman with a no-nonsense air about her came in, looking from Mrs. Rutherford to me. "I hope I'm not interrupting." Obviously she was waiting to be told who I was. Her manner was a curious blend of only half-concealed curiosity and business briskness, the shield one often finds in sentimental women who have developed a kind of second skin. I'll bet she cries over movies, I thought. She distrusts her friends, and she is taken in by con men.

Mrs. Rutherford said, "We're going to have tea in a few minutes. What is it, Rose?"

"Miss Camper said you had dismissed her without warning and that you wanted me to make out a check for three months' pay."

"That is correct," Mrs. Rutherford said quietly. "For once in her life she has got a message of mine straight."

The secretary lingered. "Does Mr. Rutherford know?"

Mrs. Rutherford's face tightened. "Surely that does not concern you, Rose."

The secretary hovered, at a loss. "Do you wish me to find you another companion?"

"Thank you, Rose, but this time I prefer to select my own. It would be so nice to choose something to please myself."

The secretary went out, looking dissatisfied and as though only the strongest control prevented her from insisting. Mrs. Rutherford turned to smile at me. Seeing the way I was examining the charming little sitting room, she asked unexpectedly,

"How does it strike you?"

"Like a mink-lined prison," I said, and could have bitten my tongue off.

She nodded. "There are times when it gets a bit overwhelming, but we won't talk about that. Tell me about yourself, Mary Ann. You don't mind my calling you Mary Ann?"

"No." The word was rather muffled. "I don't mind." But I did mind, horribly. I saw myself as I really was, deceiving this woman who was already overwrought, the balance of her mind upset by grief. I was simply exploiting her condition, perhaps even increasing the mental confusion.

The tea came, delicious China tea, with tiny paper-thin sandwiches and slices of lemon with cloves stuck in them. The cups were fragile, almost transparent, and I thought how Jimmy would have loved them. Mrs. Rutherford poured the tea, handed me a cup, and said abruptly, "Thank God you've come home. It was naughty of you to worry me so." Then some dim awareness of her mental confusion made her say, "It's delightful to have you here, Mary Ann. Tell me about yourself."

So I told her about the mother who had been a seamstress and about high school and how I hadn't been trained for anything when my mother died so I got a job as a companion. I had good references, but one of my employers had died and the other was unavailable in Switzerland. Right now I was advertising, and I described the disheartening responses I had had.

It was all too pat. I knew that. Much too pat. If she hadn't been as she was, she'd have seen through it. But there was obviously some inner turmoil; for some reason she could not accept the death of her daughter, and she was wandering in a halfway world of tortured make-believe.

She leaned forward and put a hand on mine. "I got rid of my companion today. I hated the woman. My husband chose her, but she never suited me. Sometimes she seemed to make a business of thwarting me. I want someone young and gay and pleasant to have around, someone like you. Would you care to come to me for, say, a month and try it? Of course, there's not much gaiety here, but when my daughter comes back you'll have someone young to be with."

Oops, she was off again.

"Of course, you can't blame Mary Ann for wanting to break away," she went on. "You're young only once. It's life she needs, not all this cotton wool and doctors for a perfectly healthy girl. She is a perfectly healthy girl, you know," Mrs. Rutherford assured me with dreadful earnestness, a thin hand clutching my wrist. "But this place must seem oppressive to the young."

"It seems very beautiful to me."

"Yes," she agreed. Unexpectedly she smiled and I caught a faint glimpse of the woman she had been, of the girl who must have resembled Mary Ann. "The very best butter." Then she added matter-of-factly, "People pay a heavy price for money. Before you'll be allowed to come to me they will check on your background and whether you are apt to steal the silver or are a reporter in disguise or —"

I laughed. "Or an enemy agent? Well, everyone seems to be checked on these days. It will be a novelty to me. I've never even had a questionnaire or been polled for my opinion or anything."

For a little while that dreadful vacillation went on in her troubled mind. Part of the time she confused me with her dead daughter; part of the time she saw me as myself, though even then it was as a kind of substitute Mary Ann.

Once she said, breaking off in the midst of an account of an art exhibit she had visited, "Every young girl has a right to meet young men and dance and maybe even flirt a little.

If you come to me, I shall insist that you have perfect freedom to enjoy any outside engagements you care to make, and you won't be accountable to anyone."

When I got up to leave she took both my hands in hers. "I hope you won't mind too much if — if anyone should seem impertinent. I'll never understand why being rich gives people extra privileges and the right to pry into private lives."

"Who is going to seem impertinent?"

"Probably it will be Forrest — Forrest Preston. He is a great help to my husband." She couldn't have made it clearer that she loathed the thought of the man.

On my way back to the furnished room I wrote a postcard:

> Met Mrs. Rutherford. Offered job as companion. All depends on references. Looks as though I am home free.

I addressed it to the post office box.

# 4

There was nothing for me to do now but to wait for clearance from Rutherford's henchman. My landlady had grudgingly agreed to permit me to use her telephone if I paid for my calls, but she said I would have to answer the phone myself, as she couldn't trot up and down stairs all day long. She rented two floors of an old brownstone, lived on the first floor, and sublet the second in furnished rooms. She wasn't unpleasant, just overworked and accustomed to having people walk out, taking whatever hadn't been nailed down, as she expressed it.

Three people had the number: Jimmy, Philip, and Uncle Bert, who was no relation, of course, but said he liked to have me call him uncle, not having any young people of his own. "And anyhow," he had added lazily, his eyes smiling, "it will check any lascivious tendencies on my part." Jimmy had been warned not to call from the shop or the apartment, and I set definite times when I could answer the telephone.

The night after my triumphant card to

Jimmy, Philip called promptly at six o'clock, and I ran down to answer the telephone.

"Okay, honey?" he asked, and without waiting for a reply he went on, "I picked up Jimmy's card for him this morning and I went up to see you."

"I'm sorry I missed you."

"I changed my mind because you already had company. They don't waste time, do they?"

"What do you mean?" I was aware that the kitchen door was ajar and all sounds of clatter had stopped.

"There was a guy propped outside your building, filling a pipe, and when you came out and went to that little lunchroom on the corner, he sauntered in your direction. He ate at a separate table and then, when you took a walk up Riverside Drive, he followed you. I hope," Philip added angrily, "he caught cold and has corns and develops shingles."

I laughed, but it wasn't really funny, of course. The idea that I had been followed without my knowledge made me curiously uneasy.

"Watch your step, Jennifer. I don't like any part of this."

"Well, don't upset Jimmy about it."

"Okay. Okay. But remember, whether you see him or not, there is someone checking on you and what you do and whom you meet." Trust Philip to pay attention to the dative.

"Oh," I wailed in disappointment. "I was going to have dinner with Uncle Bert to-morrow."

"I'll call it off for you. A marquis doesn't fit in with the Mary Ann Weldone back-ground. I take it you've made yourself known."

"Oh yes," I said with exaggerated enthu-siasm. "It's wonderful. I have an offer of a job as companion to a perfectly lovely woman. I'm just waiting until she can check my references."

"Overheard?" he asked quietly.

"Yes," I added with exaggerated em-phasis. "Isn't it just marvelous?"

"I could think of a lot of other words. Watch yourself, Jennifer. I must have been out of my mind when I thought this was a workable idea."

For a moment, thinking of that mink-lined prison, of the chauffeur waiting out-side Tiffany's as though Mrs. Rutherford might try to go somewhere on her own, of the unknown man who had followed me without my knowledge, I was tempted to back out. But I remembered what had happened to Jimmy and what might still happen to him.

"Did you have any luck with your own jobs today?" I asked.

There was an uneasy pause. Philip did not want to tell me, but he did not want to lie to me either. "I checked with a friend on the *Chronicle*, the paper that carried that scurrilous article about dishonest art dealers. Rutherford is part-owner."

"Uh-huh. And what about the insurance company and the lawyer who wouldn't help?"

"He's on the board of the insurance company, and when I called the lawyer's office I was told he had left the firm and gone onwards and upwards to better things in one of the Rutherford affiliates."

"I'm staying," I said.

"Promise me this, Jennifer. At the first alarm, drop everything and get the hell out."

As I didn't want to commit myself I managed to cut him short on the excuse that someone else might want to use the telephone. Before I could go back to my room, the landlady opened the kitchen door and came out, looking at me rather oddly.

"There was a gentleman here today asking about you."

"Oh?" I tried to sound indifferent, mildly puzzled, and then I exclaimed excitedly, "About the job, you mean?"

"He didn't say. Just asked what I knew about you, how long you'd been here, what you did for a living. Nice-spoken man. Asked about your friends. I said you were quiet and no trouble, that you were job-hunting but I didn't think you'd had much luck so far."

It couldn't have been better. "That's fine. I guess they are checking up on my references."

"Well, I certainly hope you get something you like. Seems to be harder all the time to get a good job. My husband has been out of work for nearly four months, and the older you get the harder it is to land anything. He gets down-hearted — and that shows, of course — when he does manage to get an interview. Employers seem to prefer the confident people rather than the competent ones. It's not hardly fair, somehow."

"I can imagine." I told her about the offer of free board and room if I would do the housework and cooking and look after three children without pay. "Oh," I said carelessly, "what did he look like, the man who was checking up on me? Was it her son I wonder?" What I had in mind was the chauffeur who had trailed Mrs. Rutherford to Tiffany's.

"Sort of tall and thin and kind of superior in a languid sort of way — a bit la-di-dah for me. Looked down his nose like one of the lions outside the public library on Forty-second Street."

I'd run down to answer the telephone without the dark glasses, which were a definite hazard on the inadequately lighted stairs. Now my landlady looked at me in surprise. "It's a shame to cover your eyes. I never would have thought green could be so pretty. And those brows. Different, somehow."

## II

I wondered how Mr. Rutherford's henchman would be able to handle my references. One woman was dead — this was true; Philip's aunt had died several years earlier — and the other was unavailable in Switzerland.

At six the next night Philip called again, this time to tell me that he had had a visit from a man calling himself Forrest Preston, inquiring about one Mary Ann Weldone for whom Philip had written a recommendation in behalf of his dead aunt.

"Incidentally, he's the man who followed you yesterday. He's a very shrewd type, Jennifer, not missing a trick. The fact that they are checking so thoroughly on you indicates that they think you could be important. He said Mrs. Rutherford was an invalid with sudden and unpredictable whims; and her husband, for her protection, found it wise to check closely on people with whom she surrounded herself. He couldn't have been nastier in a well-bred way.

"He looked down his nose at me like a camel. If you ever meet him, don't be taken in by that air of weary boredom. The man is no fool. I'll bet he could estimate within ten dollars what my suit cost and who my tailor is and what I paid for this house. I gave him a short rundown on your qualifications for the job, as reported to me by my aunt, and said I had met you only casually when you had been called in to make a fourth at bridge and that sort of thing. Very superior sort of girl.

"By the way, he is thorough. Before coming to me he had already checked with my company, because he let slip the fact that he knew how long I had worked there and mentioned the head of the firm casually as a friend of a friend."

"Guess who?" I asked.

"Whom," Philip said.

"You and Edwin Newman! How is Jimmy?"

"I think he is getting over the worst. You jolted him out of his apathy by deciding to take action. He has had the window glass replaced and some fancy grillwork put in that should prevent breakage or theft in the future. At least he is beginning to fight."

"Thank heaven for that! But the chief thing is —"

"I know. He was shocked and stunned. He's been rocked by this violence and hostility and the unjust accusations, but as a result of his discovery of Mary Ann's deception he isn't grieving. Knowing she was using him simply as an escape hatch helped cure him."

"I'd like to know who the man was — the baby's father, I mean. Do you think it was the one who came to see you?"

"God knows. On the whole I'd be inclined to say not. I wouldn't put much past him, but he didn't strike me as a seducer of retarded youth. It would take a special type of man for that, Jennifer. Not too much to say a criminal type. Oh, your Uncle Bert sends his love, and you aren't to fail to call if you need help. Apparently Mr. Bartlett lighted a fire under him before he took off for parts unknown. You've got a lot of good guys worried, Jennifer."

I was worried, too. It was one thing to try to work my way into the Rutherford household in order to clear Jimmy. It was very much another to take advantage of the heartbreak of a mother so mentally disturbed that she could not accept her daughter's death and was already beginning to confuse me with her. If Rutherford had not been so determined to destroy Jimmy, I'd have backed out then and there.

The day after that, my landlady came up to tap on my door and hand me a note. "You're to go right away," she whispered in excitement. "There's an automobile the length of a Pullman car waiting for you — and the handsomest man I've ever laid eyes on. Sort of like that George Sanders I used to drool over years ago in the movies. Uniform and everything. You've got it made, Miss Weldone."

The note had been typed on paper with Mrs. Rutherford's address engraved at the top. It said that Mrs. Rutherford had checked Miss Weldone's references, found them satisfactory, and would be happy to have her take over her duties at once. A car was being sent for her. The note was signed Rose Miller, Secretary to Mrs. Rutherford.

"Say I'll be down as soon as I have packed," I said, and the landlady scurried away, too impressed by the chauffeur and the car to object to my somewhat autocratic order.

Philip had found me a couple of second-hand suitcases, as the luggage Uncle Cliffe had given me was much too expensive — and anyhow had my initials stamped on it. I packed quickly, locked the suitcases, took a last look around, shoved on the dark glasses, and picked up my handbag.

Then I sat down suddenly, knees shaking. I had forgotten to check my bag and, sure as shooting, someone would do it. I removed my social security card and driving license with unsteady fingers. I might have to produce a social security card, but I could say I had lost mine and perhaps Philip would know how I could get a replacement with the name of Mary Ann Weldone. I seemed to be getting in deeper and deeper. Behind a mirror I found an old shopping list and a note for a hairdresser's appointment in Paris. Stuck carelessly into the billfold was Uncle Cliffe's unlisted number at the Plaza. I was aware of how close I had come to disaster, just when I was in a state of euphoria over having scaled the walls of the Rutherford fortress.

Then I opened the door, looked down the stairs, and saw the straight trim figure in the tailored uniform, saw the head of polished black hair. He turned as my door opened. He was indeed almost spectacularly handsome.

"Miss Weldone?"

"Yes, will you — ?"

"Your suitcases? Of course." He came up the stairs, collected the bags after a swift look around the shabby room, and went down to put them in the trunk of the car. By the time I had spoken to my landlady about forwarding mail, though I knew there would be nothing unless someone else wanted an employee either to work for nothing or for dubious purposes, he was waiting at the car door. As I passed him to get in, I took another look, and this time I met his eyes; hard, cynical, insolent. He was the arrogant male to his fingertips and somehow less attractive but more formidable. He was the kind to exploit women, and it was a safe guess that he had a long list of willing victims. I made up my mind to steer clear of him.

Once more I crossed Fifth Avenue under his guidance, this time, I suspected, to identify me to the doorman and the armed guard inside. Both men stared at me as I went by, memorizing me, and I realized again how miraculous had been my assault on this fortress. Without sheer chance in the form of the enterprising photographer, I'd never have managed it. One thing I was sure of, neither of those men was surprised to see me. Rutherford news traveled fast.

The same maid admitted me to the great apartment. "Miss Weldone? I'll show you to your rooms: a little suite — sitting room, bedroom, and bath on the third floor. Mrs. Rutherford left orders we were to be sure and explain that you are to ask for anything you require."

This time, instead of the circular staircase, we took a tiny elevator that held just the two of us. The suite into which she escorted me was, heaven knows, finer than anything I'd ever been accustomed to, except on those visits when I was a little girl to Lady Mary's home, but they were like any suite in a luxury hotel. Every comfort. Strictly impersonal. Completely neutral.

"Someone will unpack for you," the maid said. "Mrs. Rutherford asked me to say she'd like you to lunch with her. Lunch will be served in about twenty minutes. Meantime she thought you might like to learn your way around the apartment. There are three floors, you know, and it might be confusing to a stranger."

I tossed my coat on a chair, made sure that my dark glasses were in place, and opened the door, starting when I saw the shadow that moved away from the wall.

"Miss Weldone?" The voice was lazy. "Mrs. Rutherford suggested that I show you the way around this warren. My name is Preston — Forrest Preston."

At first sight I disliked Forrest Preston. I didn't have red hair for nothing, even though it had darkened to a kind of auburn. There was condescension in every cadence of his voice, in his expression, in his posture. Compared with him the public library lions looked like Pollyanna, the Glad Girl.

"Oh, yes," I said brightly, "you must be the man who talked to my landlady and asked questions about me."

If I had expected to take him off balance, I was mistaken. "Well, of course, it is a confidential post, isn't it? And we didn't have any luck with your references: Switzerland and the hereafter. Not too satisfactory."

Don't lose your temper, I warned myself. The man is deliberately baiting you.

So I swallowed hard and smiled and said rather weakly that these things do happen.

He grinned then. "So they do," he said appreciatively, and I knew I'd had the worst of that particular bout.

Sauntering at my side, Forrest took me over the three floors of the triplex. It was magnificent. You'd think it could supply everything anyone would want, but the mistress of the establishment had taken refuge in an escape from reality and her daughter, "the girl who had everything," had taken an overdose of sleeping pills. Recalling her final note, I found it difficult to sympathize with Mary Ann, who had left devastation in her wake.

Forrest hesitated for a moment before a door on the second floor. "These were Mary Ann's rooms." They were exquisite, but the first thing to strike me was that they had no deserted look. It would seem that Mary Ann was expected to put in an appearance at any moment. There were fresh flowers in vases, a filmy negligée was tossed over a chaise longue, there were matching satin slippers beneath, a book lay on the bedside table, and a small clock ticked away cheerfully.

Forrest watched my face. "Beautiful, isn't it?"

"It's awful," I said almost in a whisper. "Why won't Mrs. Rutherford let her die? This is surely worse for her. This obsession, this determination to believe the girl is still alive, that she just stepped out for a minute."

"Bad," he agreed, "and now, of course, with another Mary Ann . . ." He said no more, simply waited for me to precede him out of the lovely little sitting room, to which its owner would never return.

## III

Lunch was served in a small breakfast room on the first floor of the triplex, which was the twelfth floor of the building. Mrs. Rutherford came to meet me, holding out both hands. "Mary Ann! Welcome, my dear. This, as you know now, is my husband's chief assistant, Mr. Preston. But we're all going to be friends, good friends. Mary Ann, this is Forrest."

"Mary Ann," he murmured, his eyes glinting. "Well done." So it was to be battle stations right from the start. With all my heart I wished I had paid attention to Jimmy and that I were now safely in the shop while he was snatching a bite of lunch. A normal life whose only problem was a perennial lack of funds. But, I reminded myself, that was the past. Now the man Rutherford was determined to destroy the little business and Jimmy's credibility, in case he should attempt to exploit whatever explosive information Rutherford believed him to have.

There was no safety any more.

It was Mrs. Rutherford who dominated the conversation during lunch. So far as I could guess, she was not accustomed to having her own way, and her victory in acquiring me as a companion made her exultant. It was going to be a joy to have someone young in the house. There wasn't anyone young there now, except Forrest, of course, and that wasn't the same. Her voice trailed off as though she had lost track of what she was saying.

Then with an effort she pulled herself together again. It seemed to me that there was a struggle going on in her, a part of her retreating from reality, a part trying to block that retreat.

"We must do some shopping," she said happily. "I don't mean to suggest that your dress isn't nice — very nice indeed. But I do think new clothes build morale, don't you?"

Forrest said nothing. He was waiting, I knew, for me to grasp at the opportunity to get myself an expensive wardrobe for free. Instead I turned to him, smiling. "And what does the chief assistant to an important man like Mr. Rutherford do?"

"Oh, I'm the Lord High Everything Else, a snapper-of unconsidered trifles, a handyman. But at this moment, to be truthful —"

"Oh, yes." I beamed at him.

Unexpectedly his lips twitched. "I am recuperating from an operation, and Mr. Rutherford suggested I stay here until I regain my strength. Taking it easy."

Mrs. Rutherford's eyes were turned on him and then dropped to her plate.

"Still," I said sweetly, "I'll bet he can think up things for idle little hands to do."

Forrest broke out laughing.

# 5

After lunch Mrs. Rutherford said she hadn't been sleeping well and she'd try to get some rest. Anyhow, it would be nice for us "young things" to get acquainted.

Forrest followed me up to the third floor and looked around my sitting room. "Satis-factory?"

"Like the very best hotel."

"Oh, you'll change all that when you begin to fit in. I can see you are going to make yourself quite at home." Without waiting for an invitation he sat down in one of the comfortable chairs in my little sitting room. I opened my lips to protest and he said easily, "It's all right. I left the door open. Half a dozen people could hear you scream."

"Are you always this disagreeable?"

"You know what, Mary Ann? You're just looking for insults. Why don't you relax? After all, you're among friends."

He lighted a cigarette for me and sat smoking meditatively while I began to fidget. Then he started talking casually. He asked me about my mother and schooling and teachers and the friends I had made at school. He really had done his homework, but he couldn't trip me up, thank heaven. Of course, if he actually went back to the school it would be possible to find some record of me if he looked for the right class and under the right name. I'd won a scholarship to a minor college and had given it up because Jimmy needed me in the shop. I'd been captain of the girls' swimming team and there was a picture of me somewhere in their archives when I was chosen the year's prettiest girl. But that, as Jimmy had pointed out at the time, did not mean much. Anyone who wasn't actually slab-faced could have won.

All this was as easy as pie. I knew the answers and expanded on some of them, telling about the teachers I had especially liked and explaining why. As I talked, obviously relaxed and at ease, I could see that Forrest was puzzled. I was telling the truth and he knew it.

When he came to my employment as a companion I had to be more careful. Philip had briefed me about his aunt, who had been his only living relation and had left him the Fifty-eighth Street house and a pleasant income. But the friend who had gone to

Switzerland was a young woman whom I had never seen, and I had to watch my step.

But why, Forrest asked, look for a job as companion when surely there were better-paid positions with more of a future.

"It's a question of training," I explained, "or rather of no training. I had to get a job right out of high school and I wasn't equipped with office skills. Anyhow, I was lucky in the jobs I had. Both women made me feel like a part of the family. I really never knew how lucky I was until I found myself out of a job for the first time," and I told him about the discouraging responses to my ad in *The New York Times*.

"And then," I concluded, "running into Mrs. Rutherford like that. Just sheer luck."

"Apparently," Forrest said lazily, "she took one look at you and promptly fired her companion without notice."

"It wasn't a bit that way. The woman acted more like a governess with a recalcitrant child. She kept telling her employer what to do and what not to do. It was maddening. I didn't blame Mrs. Rutherford for reaching the breaking point, and that was before she even noticed me."

"Mrs. Rutherford has been in bad shape since her daughter's death, but you must have noticed her condition yourself."

I nodded. "If she could just face reality!"

"You know," Forrest said, "I'll never understand why a girl like Mary Ann should have killed herself unless she was driven to it. One thing I hope to do before I die is to find out what makes that bastard Bartlett tick. What did he do to her?"

I tried to keep my face expressionless. Obviously Forrest had not been informed of her pregnancy, which seemed to let him out as the culprit. And yet he appeared to be the only man who could have met her easily and without supervision.

"If she was unhappy in her marriage, she could always have come home, couldn't she?" I asked.

"She was restless, impatient of the kind of protection by which she was surrounded."

"Well, if you ask me, so is her mother. Fed to the teeth with the people who tell her what to do and what not to do. What that woman needs is some kind of respect for her feelings, for her wishes."

"My, my!" Forrest got out of his chair, unfolding like a jackknife, because he was very tall. And then suddenly he was serious. "You can be the saving of Mrs. Rutherford or you can be poison. If you are not totally rotten, you won't let her get confused about you being her daughter. You'll prevent her

86

from buying you clothes and — other things."

"Such as diamond bracelets?"

"Yes, damn it, diamond bracelets! If you're the kind of person Hanning says you are" — I caught my breath and then remembered that he had checked with Philip on his aunt's reference — "you could bring some life and maybe healthy cheerfulness into this mausoleum. But if I catch you trying to manipulate Mrs. Rutherford or take advantage of her in any way, you'll be sorry you were born."

"Somehow you fail to terrify me, but you bore me."

"While I'm doing that I might as well go on with what I have to say. Blackmail is a prison offense. Once convicted you'll have a criminal record that will stick for the rest of your life."

When I finally remembered to close my mouth, which was hanging wide open in sheer surprise, I said, "Will you kindly get out of my room?"

"Of course." He stood looking down at me. "Two questions and then you'll see the last of me — for a time. What's wrong with your eyes?"

"Well, I — I've had operations and my eyes are vulnerable to light. It won't last long. In a few months I'll be able to wear glasses that are just slightly tinted and in time get along without them altogether."

"It's hard to judge a person when you can't see eyes." He stared as though trying to look through the huge dark glasses, whose frames concealed over a third of my face. "Voices, of course, reveal education and breeding, but the mouth and eyes — there's nothing wrong with your mouth. Very nice indeed."

"I know now how slaves must have felt on the auction block. It's a wonder you don't examine my teeth while you're about it."

"How to make friends and influence people. What you need, Miss Weldone, is a course in how to win the popularity sweepstakes."

"Believe it or not, all I want is a chance to earn my living."

He grinned. "What was the name of that old tearjerker? Gertie the Sewing Machine Girl, or something like that. And that brings me to my second question. What are you doing here?"

"I was offered a job as companion," I said, speaking slowly and carefully as though addressing a dull child. "There's no secret about that. According to my landlady, you checked on me."

"I did?"

"Well, she described you as looking down

your nose like the lions outside the Forty-second Street library or like a camel."

His lips twitched but he managed to remain grave. I saw his eyes crinkle at the edges, and then he sobered. "Keep your wisecracks for me, Mary Ann. Don't try them on Rutherford. That's fair warning. He doesn't tolerate people who answer back. He thinks it is fatal for a man to laugh at himself, which only attracts other people's ridicule and hurts his own importance."

"My God," I said limply. "How can anyone keep sane and not laugh at himself?"

Again that look of perplexity crossed his face. "You're an odd combination, Mary Ann. Very odd."

"In what way?"

"Shall we be frank for a minute? Okay." He didn't wait for a reply. "This whole situation stinks to high heaven. You appear out of the bright blue yonder in time to smash the camera of a man taking a picture of Mrs. Rutherford, and just at the moment when she, in one of her rare flashes of independence, has broken with her companion. So — surprise, surprise — you are looking for a job as companion and can provide references from people either dead or out of reach. More surprising still, you are yclept Mary Ann."

"Must you be quaint?"

"So what is your game?" This time he waited for a reply.

I sighed loudly. "I need a job. I have to work for a living. I don't suppose you'd believe me, but I'd like to help Mrs. Rutherford. She is desperately unhappy. She asked what I thought of this place and I said it was a mink-lined prison and she said, 'The very best butter.' I suspect Mary Ann was tired of the very best butter and tired of being guarded all the time. In her place I'd have run away, too."

I stood up then, an indication I wanted him to leave. He was very close, looming over me. Then his hand darted out and snatched at my glasses. We stared at each other for a long moment and then he drew an unsteady breath.

At length he handed me the glasses. "With eyes like that you are quite right to take care of them." He turned swiftly and went out of the room.

## II

I wrote a postcard to Jimmy, saying I had the job and was settled in a pretty suite of rooms. I hadn't seen Mr. R. yet, but I had met the camel. Philip would know. I'd been escorted all over the place and could guarantee neither the missing Sisley nor the Queen Carlotta dressing table was there. I'd keep in touch. Love, Jennifer.

I put the card in my handbag and went down the stairs to the first floor, passing an open door beyond which I saw a chef in a tall white hat and, in the library, a maid dusting books.

No one seemed to notice me as I opened the door and stepped into the outside corridor to ring for the elevator, but before the door could close on me, there were running steps, a voice called, "Hold it, please," and Mrs. Rutherford's middle-aged secretary got breathlessly into the car.

"You are Miss Weldone, Mrs. Rutherford's new companion. Such a surprise to us all." She was trying to catch her breath, and she had not taken time to button her coat or pull on her gloves. Apparently the new companion was not to be allowed to leave the apartment without some supervision. And if that didn't explain Mary Ann's desperate need to escape, what did?

We went through the lobby, eyed as usual by the armed guard and the doorman. She looked across the street. "Didn't you order the car? I'll call Max. It won't take a minute."

"I don't want to drive. I just want to walk a bit and get a breath of fresh air."

"Oh, well, I'll walk with you. With my weight I really should get more exercise. Ten pounds too much." She was at least thirty pounds overweight. "Now tell me," she went on confidentially, taking my arm as though to prevent my getting away, reminding me irresistibly of the Red Queen, "what really happened? Of course, Mrs. Rutherford sometimes has vagaries, as I am sure we all do, but firing that poor woman who had been with her for four years without a moment's warning — and just picking you up, as one might say. We're all simply stunned. What really did happen?"

"I can't tell you. I caught sight of a photographer when he took a picture of her, and I thought it was a dirty trick. That's why I smashed his camera. And I didn't have anything to do with the firing of the other woman. That was done before Mrs. Rutherford even noticed me. The companion was acting as though she had a right to give the orders, and I don't blame Mrs. Rutherford for rebelling against it. How she put up with it for four years I can't imagine."

"Where —"

I pulled my arm away and dropped my card in the letter box.

Rose Miller stared after it as though trying to read it through the box. I think she would have snatched it back if she could have managed it. "You needn't do that. The mail is left on the table in the foyer and Max takes it straight to the post office every day."

Stopping on the way to enable Mr. Rutherford to read it, I thought. I said aloud, "I'm not used to all that service." I began to lengthen my stride.

She caught my arm again. "Look, I can't walk so fast."

"Then I think," deciding the time had come to assert myself, "I'll go on alone. I find a walk doesn't do me much good unless I keep up a fairly brisk pace. I'll be seeing you." I released my arm and crossed the street just as the light changed, leaving her behind. After a few blocks I found a public telephone in a drugstore on Madison Avenue and called Philip at his office. I gave him a quick résumé of the situation so far.

"Watch that guy Forrest," he told me uneasily. "He's an unknown quantity and, from what you say, he's on to you. Also he's seen your eyes."

"Well, he hasn't seen Jimmy, so no harm is done."

"Any chance that he is the guy who got Mary Ann pregnant?"

"Not a chance, I'd think. Of course I don't know. My own best bet is the chauffeur."

"The what?"

"Snob. You heard me. And he is the best-looking man I've ever seen."

"Well, if you're the kind of girl who falls for anything like that," he said, annoyed.

I laughed. "Philip, you idiot!"

"Jennifer!"

I knew that tone. In a moment he'd be telling me about the house on East Fifty-eighth Street where there was plenty of room for Jimmy, too.

"Philip, there's one thing. I don't believe Mary Ann was guarded just because of the possibility of kidnapping or because she wasn't mentally adult. Her mother is guarded the same way. Rutherford tried hard to keep them both isolated from other people. I don't know why, unless Uncle Cliffe was right and he is afraid they might talk."

"You're going a bit astray, aren't you, Jennifer?"

"What do you mean?"

"You started out to discover why Rutherford is trying to break Jimmy."

"I haven't forgotten. I wouldn't stay on a minute if it weren't for that. But I know one thing. Someone is blackmailing Mr. Rutherford, and I'm pretty sure he suspects Jimmy of doing it. And I think the camel half believes I may be in on the same game."

Philip groaned. "You might as well be a match in a powder factory. Get out while you can, Jennifer. Please, darling!"

Philip rarely allowed himself any endearments, so I know this was serious. "Not yet. If there is a blackmailer — and the camel practically accused me — it's got to be someone close to Mrs. Rutherford and to Mary Ann. And that means someone in the household. I'm going to smoke him out. Or her."

"Just let me know where to pick up the pieces," Philip said gloomily.

# 6

The question of whether the companion was expected to dine with the family was answered when, about five o'clock, a maid knocked at my sitting-room door and came in with three dresses over her arm.

"I am Hilda, Mrs. Rutherford's personal maid. This afternoon she went shopping and picked out some dresses for you. Size twelve. They will probably need shortening, so if you'll decide which one you want to wear tonight, I'll take up the hem."

They were all lovely, and I selected a soft blue with long sleeves, a round neck, and a skirt that, when taken up, just brushed the carpet. With my eyes and hair, as I had learned long ago, my choice of colors was strictly limited. No reds or pinks. Blue and green and brown and gray were safest.

I had not been in the place more than a few hours and already I was accepting expensive gifts from my warm-hearted employer but, though I dreaded Forrest's sardonic and contemptuous eyes, there was no way to refuse the dresses without ungraciousness, if not actual rudeness.

Hilda pinned the skirt efficiently. "I'll just run up the hem. It won't take any time at all. Dinner is at eight o'clock and cocktails at seven-thirty. Usually cocktails are served in the library, and Mr. Rutherford likes people to be prompt." She gave me a quick, half conspiratorial look, and I nodded. Here at least was someone who was willing to lend me a helping hand.

By six-thirty I was ready, except for the dress, and, wrapped in my wool robe, I squatted before the low bookshelves, whistling softly to myself. The books looked as though they had come out of the ark: *Lavender and Old Lace*, *Dorothy Vernon of Haddon Hall*, *Graustark*, *The Masquerader*. Each had the name Mary Ann Rutherford written in a child's unformed hand, and I wondered why the girl's favorite reading had been relegated to a guest suite.

The shelves were deep and, when I pulled out a book with a frontispiece by Charles Dana Gibson, I noticed that behind these early twentieth-century novels there was a second row. This proved to be as nice a selection of pornography as you'd want to see. Apparently there had been more facets to Mary Ann's personality than I had realized. Whoever the man was who had corrupted her, he had made use of all the tools at hand, for I could not imagine Mary Ann, guarded as she had been, managing to buy these books for herself. I began to understand Jimmy's loathing of the man who had found an easy victim in the girl with a twelve-year-old's mentality.

When Hilda returned with the dress, she insisted on helping me slide it over my head and zipped it up for me. "It could have been made for you. What a pity you have to wear those glasses."

"Only a few more months," I said, but when I studied myself in the long mirror I agreed that it was a pity to wear those disfiguring glasses. However I wasn't there to look nice. I was there to find out why Jimmy was being hounded — and to stop it if I could.

I preferred walking down the stairs to taking an elevator. The longer I could postpone my first meeting with Mr. Rutherford, the better I liked it. I had assured myself somewhat hollowly, that I wasn't afraid of him, but I didn't make much of a success of it.

There were voices in the library, where I found Forrest, looking sleek in black tie, pouring a glass of sherry for Mrs. Rutherford, who had taken great pains with her dress — a long brown velvet that was stamped Paris in every line and matched her hair. She wore a diamond necklace, and her throat and shoulders, I noticed, seemed much younger than her face.

As I came in, Forrest looked me over, not missing a thing, and indicated the tray. "What's yours?"

"Dry sherry, please."

Mrs. Rutherford looked at the dress. "That's the one I hoped you would wear. It's wonderful with that auburn hair."

"It is quite the prettiest dress I ever had. You've been awfully kind."

"Nonsense. You have no idea how much I enjoyed getting you those dresses. It's such a long time since I've bought clothes for a girl." She started nervously, spilling a little sherry, sopping it up with her cocktail napkin.

Then Forrest said pleasantly, "Good evening, sir, are you having your usual?" and he reached for a bottle of Scotch.

"Good evening, Sarah. Forrest. And this, I assume . . ."

"This," Mrs. Rutherford said with a shade of defiance, "is Mary Ann Weldone."

"Good evening, Miss Weldone." Rutherford took up a position in front of the fireplace. No one ever looked less like The Man of Distinction. He was below middle height and he had a paunch. His eyes were like poached eggs, his lips so thin that they were almost invisible. I would have expected to find a face like his on a "Wanted" poster instead of lording it in this immense apartment, surrounded by all the appurtenances of wealth and power. He was completely out of place. I wondered what had persuaded Mrs. Rutherford, who was obviously old Boston, to marry this man who lacked every physical attraction, had no social graces, and of whom she was obviously afraid.

"Good evening," I said coolly, and I took a sip of sherry. I had to suppress a grin. It wasn't good sherry, just a cheap domestic brand. Jimmy always had excellent wines. Absurd that such a trifle helped give me back my self-confidence and take away my momentary fear.

I remembered an old acquaintance of Philip's who inherited a lot of money and built a lavish establishment. He loved the things that made a display, but he was curiously penurious about things he thought people wouldn't spot. His exquisite Venetian glass perfume bottles were filled with Coca Cola, and his vast gardens were planted with artificial flowers so he could dispense with a gardener.

I caught a somewhat puzzled look on Forrest's face and knew he was wondering what had suddenly amused me. He was watching me like a hawk. "So you are my wife's latest whim," Rutherford said. "I understand she met you for the first time — at Tiffany's, wasn't it? — and instantly discharged her old and tried companion and offered you the job on the spot."

Mrs. Rutherford put down her glass, which rattled as she set it on the table. "I never liked the woman, Paul; she was always the one who gave the orders. And Mary Ann is such a dear girl."

"I would prefer to have her called Miss Weldone. For me, at least, the other name has rather poignant associations."

That was deliberately cruel, and I wondered just how poignant the associations had been for Mary Ann, who had broken away from her father's stranglehold in her desperate search for freedom. When Jimmy had said she hated her father, he had seemed overwrought, but I could believe it now. Mr. Rutherford would be easy to hate.

"Paul!" Mrs. Rutherford made a little imploring gesture, as though trying to placate him, and suddenly I was furiously angry. Why don't you pick on someone your own

101

size, damn you, I thought, and anger helped me shake off my fear of the man, though I knew then that his antagonism toward me was something that nothing could change.

"So you met at Tiffany's." He shook his glass so that the ice tinkled against the side. "A favorite haunt of yours?"

I forced a laugh, which sounded artificial as all polite laughter does. "Good heavens, no. I'd never been inside before, but I'd always longed to see what the place was like."

"And you and the enterprising photographer just — uh — happened to — uh — converge on my wife at the same time. It was fortunate for my wife, who dislikes publicity."

Again I saw her eyes rise to his face and fall again.

"Indeed, I might say it was fortunate for both of you."

Forrest had settled himself in a deep armchair, a martini glass held between long fingers, surveying us through sleepy eyes. I was too angry to speak; I knew my voice would betray me. So the idea was that the whole thing had been a put-up job: the photographer, the smashed camera, and me in the role of the marines to the rescue. In a way it seemed preposterous that the only pure coincidence in the whole affair was the one to arouse suspicion.

Mrs. Rutherford said a little breathlessly, "It was certainly lucky for me. It was marvelous the way Mary Ann smashed that camera."

"Marvelous timing," Rutherford commented. "I assume that you will be expected to pay for the damage, Sarah. And I understand that, in spite of my explicit orders, you purchased a diamond bracelet for Mary Ann. I should dislike embarrassing you by having to cancel your credit, my dear, but this obsession must be controlled."

She pushed back her chair. "If you will excuse me a few minutes — I won't keep dinner waiting."

When she had gone, Rutherford, still posing in front of the fireplace like Stout Cortez surveying the Pacific, said, "My wife, as you may have heard, has suffered a tragic loss in the death of our only child. The blow has shattered her nervous system for the time being, and she should not be subjected to any emotional strain. She has, as you may have observed — you seem to be a very observant young woman — become somewhat erratic, discharging a faithful companion at a moment's notice and impulsively selecting a total stranger to take her place — someone about whom we know nothing."

"But surely by this time," I said, "you must know just about all there is to know about me. You have my references, which Mr. Preston checked. He has even checked with my landlady and looked up my high school yearbook."

Forrest made a quick gesture and was still again.

"The problem is," Rutherford said, "that my wife's nervous system is too shattered for her to be left in the care of strangers."

"Well, from what I saw of that companion, she acted more like a jailer. She wouldn't let Mrs. Rutherford do anything she wanted. If she had worked for me, I'd have got rid of her the first day — unless I hadn't any choice in the matter."

Rutherford's eyes flickered at that. He didn't like it any more than he liked me, which was not at all. "You are a very out-spoken young woman. If my wife's companion appeared to be firm, it is because of her emotional problems at this time; they have naturally affected her judgment. Oh, that reminds me." He held out his hand. "You must realize that in buying a bracelet for our dead daughter my wife was performing an irresponsible action. Will you give it to me, please?"

I stared at him blankly. "But I don't have

it. The clerk gave it to Mrs. Rutherford."

"And she didn't give it to you?"

"Well, of course not."

His hard eyes searched my face. Apparently he believed me, because he nodded. "Very well. But when — or if — Sarah should make you a present of the bracelet, I trust to your — uh — common sense to bring it to me at once. You could not dispose of it, you know, without a great deal of risk."

I was too taken aback to be able to answer, and he seemed to be satisfied that he had forestalled any attempt on my part to cash in on his wife's aberrations. And then I remembered Forrest's word: blackmail. So Rutherford, too, suspected that I might be in on some blackmail scheme. And within a few minutes of meeting him I found it easy to believe that there was plenty of material for any blackmailer to draw on.

Mrs. Rutherford came back and sat down with a half apologetic smile. She reached for her glass of sherry and overturned it. "How careless of me!"

"Just nerves," Rutherford said. "Nerves, Sarah. I'll call Dr. Reynolds in the morning and have him take a look at you."

The color drained out of her face, making the careful makeup conspicuous against the pale skin. Her eyes were wide with fright.

105

"Oh, Paul! Please! Please!"

"Now don't be absurd." There was a warning under the quiet voice. "He is an excellent physician."

"He'll put me in that horrible place. Don't let him, Paul!"

"Quiet, my dear." He took her hand in his and crushed it until she winced with pain, his eyes steady on her poor raddled face. "It's these emotional upsets that do you such harm."

The butler said, "Dinner is served," and Rutherford released his wife's hand and stood back to let us precede him into the dining room.

## II

Dinner was excellent and perfectly served but, except for Rutherford, I don't think any of us ate much. Mrs. Rutherford barely pretended. I pushed food around on my plate after helping myself to the minimum from each dish. Most of the conversation was between Rutherford and Forrest, who discussed the names released that day of the new president's appointments.

"That reminds me, Sarah, that the president is submitting my name as ambassador to the Court of St. James." He rolled the phrase on his lips as though tasting it.

I wondered why a man with his vast power wanted such an appointment, and looked again at the tough, gross face. Perhaps he was seeking to command a social acceptance he had so far failed to acquire.

"It occurs to me," Forrest said, "that it would be useful to have a few social ties in England, as well as your purely business associates, before you get there. I happen to know that the Marquis of Glydes is in New York, staying at the Plaza. A very useful man to know, *persona grata* everywhere. His social backing would be an 'open sesame.' "

"I thought the family was bankrupt, had to sell out everything. Matter of fact, a colleague of mine has purchased Glydes Park."

So Rutherford was hand in glove with a big Arab oil man. That information might interest the men who confirmed appointments.

"The Glydes' social position was never for sale." Forrest's eyes flickered in my direction because I had dropped my butter knife with a little crash on the plate when I heard Uncle Bert's name.

"Impoverished nobility doesn't carry much weight anywhere," Rutherford said. "Still you never know when a contact may be useful. And a marquis, after all . . ."

"Quite," Forrest said. "I'll get in touch with the man who saw him and arrange something casual."

"No sense in pussyfooting. Let Glydes know there would be something in it for him."

"No," Forrest said so emphatically that Rutherford let the suggestion drop.

After dinner Mrs. Rutherford excused herself with the explanation of a raging headache. There was, she assured her husband tremulously, nothing else wrong with her.

Rutherford was not a man to let an opportunity slip. "Reynolds will be able to spot all that." He got up. "I'll have my coffee in the study. You might join me there, Forrest, when you've finished. But take your time." Apparently he was priming Forrest to see what he could get out of me.

When Rutherford had gone I turned to Forrest. "Can't you stop it?"

"Stop what?"

"Stop Mr. Rutherford driving his wife mad."

"That sounds like an effective second-act curtain."

"This is not funny. It's grim and it's terrible. That poor woman! As though it hadn't been bad enough for her to lose her daughter. Think of the way she is treated. This place is a prison. She is watched all the time. She isn't allowed to do anything by herself. Probably everyone in the place is hired by her husband."

"For her protection," Forrest said lightly, his eyes watching me.

"Was it for her daughter's protection, too? Why did she have to run away?"

The coffee tray had been set before me. I told the butler that Mr. Rutherford would have his in the study and poured Forrest's. "Sugar?" I asked.

"Butlers don't fluster you. You've been around a lot for a paid companion."

"Oh, I worked for the best people. Not the richest, just those with good manners and decent attitudes toward each other. Not thugs dressed up in dinner jackets. I will never understand why so many men of great wealth are so darned ordinary."

"Perhaps because acquisitiveness is not an extraordinary quality. So you aren't impressed by our tycoon. By the way, what amused you so before dinner?"

"That cheap sherry." I found myself laughing.

"Aren't you afraid I'll tell the great man what your opinion is?"

I was surprised to hear myself say, "No, I'm not. I don't like you one bit, but I don't think you are a sneak. But if you stand aside and let Mrs. Rutherford be destroyed, you are absolutely contemptible."

"How to make friends," Forrest murmured.

"This isn't a popularity contest."

He burst out laughing and held his cup for a refill. "A penny for them," he said.

"What was Mary Ann like?"

"That's a dangerous subject here," he said soberly. "Keep away from it." He finished his coffee and got up. "His master's voice. Parting is such sweet sorrow."

I went up to my sitting room and wrote a note to Philip, asking him to find out about Dr. Reynolds, his professional standing, and what could be learned about "that horrible place" that had so frightened Mrs. Rutherford. I said I was afraid Mr. Rutherford was planning to have his wife shut up, and if he succeeded it might drive her permanently out of her mind.

"Try to find out as soon as you can," I added. "That poor, poor woman."

I added a postscript. "By the way, Mr. R. has wangled an appointment as ambassador to Great Britain. I can't imagine why he wants it, as he has such big business interests. He may try to get in touch with — or he'd say contact — Uncle Bert for his social backing. I nearly jumped out of my skin when the camel suggested him. You'd better warn him."

I addressed the envelope. There were no stamps in the otherwise well-equipped desk. Evidently no one was supposed to mail his own letters. So I slipped mine under the blotter. I'd mail it myself in the morning.

# 7

That night I lay awake for a long time trying to put together the chain of events that had brought me to where I was with such fantastic ease, almost as though the way had been prepared for me. I had learned a lot: that Mrs. Rutherford was more than a trifle disturbed mentally and that her condition was being worsened by her husband, whether deliberately or not. Her attitude toward me was ambivalent. She liked me for myself, but somewhere in her poor muddled head she confused me with her lost Mary Ann. Part of her mind knew her daughter was dead; part of it refused to accept the fact.

Forrest, the camel, was perfectly aware that I was playing a game of my own, and yet he had not — I was sure of this — betrayed me to Mr. Rutherford, at least up to this point. A good sign? But he refused to intervene on behalf of Mrs. Rutherford. A bad sign?

I awakened in the night with the impression that a light had been flashed on my face, but the bedroom was dark, as was my sitting room beyond. Something creaked in the sitting room and then there was silence. Just the unaccustomed sounds of an unfamiliar dwelling I told myself. In an establishment so closely guarded there was nothing to fear. I fell asleep again.

In the morning Mrs. Rutherford's maid came into my bedroom, where I was enjoying breakfast in bed, an unaccustomed luxury.

"Good morning, Miss Weldone. Madame wondered whether you would be good enough to read the morning paper to her in about half an hour."

"Of course. I'll be happy to."

Hilda was looking at me curiously, and I realized that I wasn't wearing the dark glasses. I groped on the bedside table and slipped them on.

"Oh, and Miss Miller is collecting the mail for Max. Have you anything to go out?"

I remembered the secretary's interest in the postcard I had mailed the day before and my impression that she would have snatched it out of my hand if she could. "Nothing today, thank you, Hilda."

When I had showered and dressed in a gray flannel sports suit with a green scarf tucked into the throat and deep pockets in the jacket, I went out to the sitting room to pick up my letter. It wasn't there.

I lifted the blotter, looked in the drawers, on the carpet, in the wastebasket. It was gone. So someone in the house had taken the letter and knew its contents — knew that I was trying to interfere in Rutherford's projects for his wife. Forrest, if it was Forrest, would recognize the reference to the camel. Well, the fat was in the fire. I had bungled everything. All I could do now was take Philip's advice and get out. Now that my cover had been blown by my own carelessness, there was nothing left for me to do.

Mrs. Rutherford was in her dressing room, a fantastic place with mirrored walls that looked like something out of a Hollywood set in the lush days of the movies. I was sure she had never planned it herself.

She smiled at me when I answered her summons to come in. "How nice you look, after Old Sourpuss! I like young things about me." She broke off. Then she said, "Perhaps you will be good enough to read the paper. My former companion made everything sound like a stock report or a page out of the *World Almanac*."

She was in a curious mood, and it took me a moment to get my emotional bearings. It seemed to me as though she half believed she and I shared a secret, the secret of my real identity. Somewhere in her clouded mind persisted the idea that I was really her own Mary Ann. It was terrible and it was heartbreaking. To connive at this deception would be horrible, but to undeceive her would be brutal. I'd never been so torn in all my life as to what course of action to follow.

Hilda was giving her mistress a manicure and I was aware of her curious eyes, which seemed to be multiplied in all the mirrors. I opened *The New York Times*, took a minute to adjust to reading with dark glasses, and began picking headlines at random, as I had no idea of what interested her.

"No war," she protested. "No war! The ultimate stupidity of mankind. And no politics, please. With Paul steeped night and day for months in fund-raising for the campaign, I need a change of pace."

I flipped pages and found a story about a royal scandal, to which she listened avidly. She began to discuss it, speculating. "Of course, when Paul is ambassador we'll probably meet all these people. What bothers me most is the protocol. Who has precedence over whom? I'd never know how to seat a formal dinner party. I suppose I could ask Forrest to help me. He is a mine of information and so presentable — good background and family and education. And nice manners, of course, though too much of the Cabots and the Lodges. My family is Back Bay, but Forrest was really born to the purple. Paul always hoped he and Mary Ann would make a match of it, but somehow they didn't seem to take to each other."

Her eyes flickered to my face, then flickered away again, as though she had touched her finger to my lips. It was eerie.

She switched back to the royal scandal and I listened with half an ear, scanning columns in search of something else to interest her.

## ART DEALER MUGGED

James Monk Bartlett, husband of Mary Ann Rutherford, who died of an overdose of sleeping pills three months after their secret marriage, was found in Madison Square Park early this morning. He had been mugged and attacked with a knife. One arm was badly slashed and he suffered a slight chest wound. He was taken to a hospital where, on regaining consciousness, he said he had not seen his attackers. He had been walking because he found it difficult to sleep. He will be released today.

"Don't you agree, my dear?" Mrs. Rutherford said in a raised voice, and I realized that she had spoken before. I met her impatient eyes in the mirror and nodded. "No," she said to Hilda, "I don't like that polish. Just the faintest pink."

She turned to smile at me. "And what would you like to do today?" she asked happily.

"Let's go out somewhere," I suggested. Anywhere, away from listening ears, watching eyes. And somehow I had to get in touch with Philip and find out about Jimmy and tell him about the missing letter. And I had to warn Uncle Bert of that projected invasion by the Rutherford forces. But one thing that newspaper story had done: it had made me determined to stay on, whatever the risk, and dig out the source of Jimmy's persecution. I was frantic to see with my own eyes that he was all right. He had always neglected himself and now, if ever, he would need some kind of sensible care.

"Let's do some shopping," Mrs. Rutherford suggested.

"Why don't we go to the Metropolitan Museum?" I countered, unwilling to let Forrest or Rutherford feel I was exploiting her generosity and thereby perhaps cause her husband to take away her charge accounts and inflict embarrassment on her. "It's practically across the street, and we could just stroll over. We needn't use the car." And that, I thought, would take care of the ubiquitous Max.

## II

The arrival of Dr. Reynolds as we were leaving the apartment came as an unpleasant surprise to Mrs. Rutherford. He was rather stout, with an unexpectedly soft voice, undistinguished features, and bifocals that kept slipping down his stubby nose, which had no bridge. He was constantly pushing them back, and the gesture had become so automatic that he was unconscious of it.

Mrs. Rutherford stopped short and clutched at my arm. The doctor gave me a careful scrutiny and then turned smiling to his reluctant patient. What he might lack in medical lore he more than made up in bedside manner. He had enough for half a dozen doctors.

"We are just going out," Mrs. Rutherford said breathlessly.

"Then I am glad I was fortunate enough to catch you in time." His tone was jovial and he seemed totally unaware of her obvious terror of him. He nodded dismissal to me and, though I wanted to protest, there was really nothing I could do. I had to stand helplessly while he led Mrs. Rutherford back to her rooms. There was no fight in her. She went with dragging feet, but she went.

After a moment's hesitation I continued on my way and only when I was out of the apartment, out of the building, drew a long breath of relief.

Thinking of my lost letter, I went over to Madison and found the drugstore from which I had made my call the day before. Armed with a handful of silver, I entered the first unoccupied booth and dialed. Philip, I was told, had not come in that morning. Would I care to leave a message? But I couldn't have him call the Fifth Avenue apartment.

I had been so sure that he would know what I should do that I felt frustrated. He was the only one who could tell me about Jimmy and how seriously he had been hurt. I knew that as soon as he saw that newspaper item he'd be hot on Jimmy's trail. That the mugging had been a coincidence I did not for one minute believe. It had been part of a deliberate campaign.

There must be someone to help me. At

length I got out the ragged Manhattan telephone directory, its pages torn and disfigured, and found the Plaza number. I had destroyed Uncle Cliffe's private number, but there would be no harm in using the switchboard.

Uncle Bert's familiar voice said, "Glydes here."

"Oh, Uncle Bert!"

"Here," he said in alarm, "what is wrong, Jennifer?"

I poured out a jumbled story, breaking off to drop more coins into the hungry maw of the telephone and hold the receiver away from my ear until the ugly jangling stopped.

There was silence when I had finally come to the end, and I said anxiously, "Uncle Bert, are you there?"

"Just thinking, my dear. Just thinking. Of course, Cliffe briefed me about your intentions before he left. I can't say I took them seriously until . . ."

"Well?"

"Your friend Philip Hanning called me this morning. He had seen a newspaper item about Jimmy being mugged — you read about that? — yes, well, he went to the hospital to pick him up. He decided, very sensibly I think, to take Jimmy to his own house, and he has sent his man Jenks to the shop to keep an eye on it until Jimmy is ready to return."

"Bless Philip! He never fails, does he? Was Jimmy seriously hurt?"

"His arm is rather badly torn, and I suppose it is painful. It will probably leave a scar. Fortunately the chest wound is trivial. He lost some blood. Hanning's housekeeper is going to look after him. Hanning hoped you would call me when you couldn't reach him at his office. The most important thing now is you, my dear, and your own safety. That stolen letter has blown your cover. The sooner you get out of your gilded cage the better."

"And what is going to happen to Mrs. Rutherford?" I demanded.

"Nothing that you can prevent. You have no authority at all." Uncle Bert sounded uncharacteristically firm about that.

"And I've involved you by the letter I lost. I'm terribly sorry."

"Now that depends," Uncle Bert said thoughtfully. "Let's suppose I am involved. Apparently Rutherford would like to use me as a sort of wedge to force open social doors. He isn't apt to do anything to endanger that, you know. Why not trust me to cope with the invading hordes, and I assure you I'm no pushover, my dear. You've done your bit. Be sensible and go up to Hanning's house. Heaven knows that you'd be welcome, from all I can gather, and you'd be able to keep an eye on Jimmy."

"And let Rutherford continue to harass Jimmy and destroy that poor woman? He's afraid of someone, Uncle Bert, and I feel pretty sure he honestly believes Jimmy is his blackmailer. If I could prove to him —"

"How?" One syllable, but it stopped me cold.

At last I said in a small voice, "Then what should I do?"

"I told you. Go up to Hanning's house and stay there."

"Just — give up then?"

This time it was Uncle Bert who was stopped cold. Glydes weren't the type to give up.

"Anyhow," I pointed out, "I can't go on taking and taking from Philip when I haven't anything but gratitude to give in return."

"He seems to be a nice fellow."

"The nicest I know. Only . . ."

"Are you temporarily off the leash?" Uncle Bert asked after a pause.

"I think so. Mrs. Rutherford and I were planning to go to the Metropolitan when the doctor came. I don't see how anyone could have followed me."

"Meet me in the Plaza lobby at one. Can you fill in the time until then? I have a few things to do in the meantime. We'll lunch and thrash things out. But unless you are sure you are in the clear, perhaps, on second thought, you had better keep away from Hanning's house, because Jimmy is in no condition to defend himself, and after Hanning goes back to work there will be no one in the house but Mrs. Jenks. Her husband, as I told you, is now at the shop. He won't, of course, attempt to sell anything. He'll simply hold off marauders."

I spent a happy hour browsing at Brentano's, because it was too chilly for window shopping, and then walked up to the Plaza. It was a typical bleak November day with a gray sky, but the store windows were bright and gay with Christmas decorations, which seem to appear earlier every year, and the throngs on the avenue were the usual New York mélange of color, race, language, and costume, all — to the casual eye, at least — part of a harmonious whole.

I waited in the lobby of the Plaza until time to meet Uncle Bert, using as a shield a paperback novel I had bought. Now and then I took a cautious look around, but no one seemed to be paying any attention to me.

I saw Uncle Bert before he recognized me, because he wasn't prepared for the huge dark glasses. I stood up and seized his arm.

"Uncle Bert!"

Like Lady Mary, his sister, he was tall and slender. He was gray, much grayer than when I had seen him last, and there were more lines in his face, but nice lines, lines of laughter at the corners of his eyes and mouth. His suit was beautifully tailored but somewhat shabby.

He smiled. "How this makes me think of a Hitchcock film!" he said happily. "That disguise. I had no idea that the situation could be so amusing."

"It isn't," I said grimly. "Not with what happened to Mary Ann and what is happening to Jimmy and his shop — and what may happen to Mrs. Rutherford."

"What you need," he diagnosed, leading me toward a dining room, "is a cocktail."

The head waiter showed us to a table and, with a flourish, presented us each with an enormous menu, took our orders for cocktails, which he retailed to a waiter, and left us after murmuring that the poached salmon was unusually fine today.

Uncle Bert, whose experience with women I assumed to be fairly extensive, waited for the cocktail to get in its work before he said, "Now then, Jennifer —" He broke off. "What's wrong?"

"The camel," I said helplessly.

Three tables away, Forrest Preston sat studiously reading a menu. At the exactly right moment he looked up, caught my eye, and got to his feet. He took one look at Uncle Bert and came to our table, smiling.

"Mary Ann! What a pleasant surprise. And — why it's Lord Glydes, isn't it? How long — it must be several years since we've met."

For sheer effrontery that took the cake.

Uncle Bert stood up, accepted Forrest's hand, and murmured, "What a coincidence."

That wiped the smile off Forrest's face. For the first time I saw him taken aback. Color rose in his cheeks, much to my delight. And then Uncle Bert surprised me. "Why don't you join us, Mr. — uh — I seem to have forgotten your name in the interval since we met."

Forrest joined us, looking as though he had expected one more step and had come down too heavily. Uncle Bert was amused. After my first moment of horror I saw that he had been quite right. There was no earthly sense in pretending that the meeting was an accidental one. Uncle Bert was putting his cards on the table, and I began to suspect that he was the better player.

"Now," he said briskly, "suppose we clear away all the debris and start with the fact that you and I have never met before. Did you come to the table to make my acquaintance in the hope of assisting your employer's social ambitions, or are you checking up on — uh —" For a moment he forgot the name I had assumed.

Forrest recuperated with lightning speed from this frontal attack. "Well, sir, at the moment she is calling herself Mary Ann Weldone." And that was trumping Uncle Bert's card with a vengeance. "However, to answer your question, I am working in my employer's interests."

"And just what does that entail?" Uncle Bert asked.

"At the moment I was trying to figure out a diplomatic way of meeting you."

"And for the long range?"

"I am attempting to run down a black-mailer."

"And you suspect this young lady?"

"Well," Forrest admitted, "I've tried. Heaven knows she has a talent for building suspicion against herself, but I can't manage it. I can see her" — and his eyes flickered toward my fingers curled around my cocktail glass — "hurling that glass in my face." Hastily I set it down. "But I can't see her working behind my back. So what she is up to defeats me."

Uncle Bert looked from one to the other, as though he were assimilating a new idea. "I find mysteries delightful in fiction but disturbing in real life. Suppose I set you straight, Mr. — uh — Let me make you known to Jennifer Bartlett, sister of the man who married Mary Ann Rutherford, the man whom Rutherford is systematically trying to destroy. Like yourself, Miss Bartlett is trying to run down a blackmailer. As for my own position, I am a kind of deputy uncle, acting for my brother-in-law, Radcliffe Bartlett. A little clearing of the air should prevent both of you from wasting your energy. And now, perhaps, Jennifer, you will oblige me by removing those offensive glasses. They serve no further purpose," Uncle Bert leaned back in his chair and smiled blandly.

# 8

When we had finished lunch and Uncle Bert had signed the check, he said, "I suggest we adjourn to my rooms upstairs — or rather my brother-in-law's rooms."

Once in the familiar living room I went first, as usual, to the windows to look at that fabulous view of Central Park, bleak now the leaves had fallen, but with the pattern of paths and lakes clearer than in the summertime, and the apartment buildings on Fifth Avenue and Central Park West looking handsome and impressive.

Before settling down I asked permission to call Philip's house and speak to Mrs. Jenks. In a few moments Jimmy took the phone away from her. He was fine, he insisted, and it was absurd for Philip to have dragged him off to his house.

"I wouldn't have come if I hadn't been weak as a cat and worried out of my head about you."

"You needn't be," I assured him. "I'm with Uncle Bert right now."

"Thank God for small blessings! But this

attack on me settles it, Jen. Drop this thing and get out of there while you are still in one piece. Philip doesn't think much of that setup, and he distrusts the guy who trailed you and checked up with him on your letters of recommendation."

"The camel," I said. "By the way, he is here now. He is Rutherford's right-hand man and he is trying to run down a blackmailer. He thought you might be it."

"What!" Jimmy yelped.

"Or that we are in it together."

"I'll be damned. I'm getting out of here and I'll see Rutherford myself."

"You will stay where you are," I told him. "Don't be stupid, Jimmy. The camel has changed his mind, I think. Or maybe he is just playing up to Uncle Bert for his own ends." I rather enjoyed that, and I could practically feel the listening silence in the room behind me.

"You are up to your usual tricks, Jen," Jimmy said in a tone of resignation. "Playing with that man like a cat with a mouse. One of these days you are going to meet your match and some maddened male will give you your comeuppance."

"I thought you didn't stoop to the use of clichés," I said loftily.

"What I'd like to do is wring your neck,"

he told me. "You never have had the slightest sense of self-preservation. What you need is masculine protection. Why don't you marry Philip and put him out of his misery?"

"If I married Philip he'd be even more miserable," I assured him.

When I set down the telephone I turned to find the two men staring at me fixedly, Uncle Bert in some amusement, Forrest with an expression I couldn't make out.

It was Uncle Bert who said, "Do let me try to clear the air of all the futile suspicions and unanswered questions beclouding this unsavory situation. Let's get the questions out and answer them, if we can."

"All right," said Forrest, looking as though he were trying to see right into my mind. "I'll start the ball rolling. Why did Mary Ann kill herself three months after she married your brother?"

"You are asking the wrong question," I said. "Why did she ask him to marry her two weeks after she first met him, practically the only man — or next to the only man — she had a chance to meet?"

"That," Forrest said, "is a question no one except your brother can answer."

"I can answer it. And so can Mr. Rutherford. He, like Jimmy, saw the autopsy report. She was pregnant when she married Jimmy, though he had never laid eyes on her until the day they met in a stalled elevator. When I saw the setup at the Rutherford apartment and realized how restricted her movements had been and how few men she had a chance to meet, I thought you must be the father."

Forrest seemed to rise by a kind of levitation out of his chair and sink back again. "Are you sure? I mean about the pregnancy?"

"Jimmy saw the autopsy report. He was stunned. Obviously she married him because she didn't know what else to do."

"But what about the man who was responsible? Look here, Mary Ann — uh, Jennifer — I never laid a hand on that girl. No credit to me. She wasn't a whole lot above the moron level, in spite of packing a lethal charge of sex appeal, which made her as dangerous as a cobra. The fact that she wasn't aware of it didn't help. But I'd seen her on and off for some months when I was spending a lot of time at the Rutherford apartment working on the presidential campaign as a combination of public relations man, private investigator, fund raiser, and what have you. Frankly, though she was a pretty girl, she bored the life out of me. It took about one week to discover that Rutherford was deliberately throwing us together, and from then on I watched my step. I didn't want a child wife, and I didn't want Rutherford for a father-in-law."

"All right," I said impatiently, "so it wasn't you. Somehow I couldn't see you in the role of gay seducer. You'd have been too busy concentrating on how superior you were."

Uncle Bert coughed.

"You make me think," Forrest retaliated, "of Benedick's words about Beatrice and the man fortunate enough not to marry her end 'scape a predestinate scratch'd face.' "

Uncle Bert's cough seemed to get worse.

"It's nice to be appreciated," I said. "And now that you have so honorably established your innocence —"

"Not so honorably," Forrest said evenly. "Mary Ann was a sweet, innocent kid, and there's no excuse for talking about her as I've been doing. She didn't know anything about the real world."

"Oh yeah?" I told him about the hidden shelf of pornography and he whistled.

"The fact remains," Uncle Bert said, "that there was a man, though you have both stressed the difficulties of anyone meeting Mary Ann. What I can't figure out is why he didn't marry her. She was heiress to a great fortune, after all."

"Was she?" Forrest said oddly. "I'd be inclined to doubt that Rutherford ever intended to leave a fortune to his daughter. He knew as well as anyone, certainly better than a comparative stranger like myself, that she was unfit to handle money, or indeed to cope with responsibility of any kind. Anyhow . . ."

When he had been silent for some time, I said abruptly, "Why was she afraid of doctors? Jimmy told me that she was terrified of them."

"Was she? I didn't know. Of course, she had been hospitalized for several months shortly before I met her. I never heard of anyone who likes hospitals, and she was so childish —"

"That horrible place," I said.

"What?"

"Mrs. Rutherford said that last night. Remember? 'That horrible place.' When her husband threatened to call Dr. Reynolds — and he did, too. The doctor came this morning and prevented her from coming out with me. She said he would put her in that horrible place. You must have heard her. She was frantic."

"Yes, but — my God! I believe there could be something in it! No one ever mentioned where Mary Ann had been or what was wrong with her, but I'm fairly sure now she had been in some private hospital run by Dr. Reynolds. When I first met her she certainly didn't give the impression of a convalescent. She was a healthy girl if I ever met one. I wonder —" And Forrest broke off, grappling with a new idea. "Someone had to provide her with those sleeping pills. She must have taken a whopping dose. If it was Dr. Reynolds — but I assumed . . ."

"You assumed that it was Jimmy," I said heatedly.

"Well, what would you have assumed?" he countered, goaded by my attitude. "At least, based on the information I had? The girl meets this guy who runs a small antiques business and he marries her in two weeks. In three months she kills herself. And just about the time of that secret marriage someone starts to blackmail Rutherford."

"You can assume a lot, it seems to me. Yesterday you were assuming that I was the blackmailer."

"Okay. Okay. But anything less likely than that accidental meeting between you and Mrs. Rutherford — and you just happening to be looking for a job as companion, and with a couple of phony references. Damn it, the whole thing stank."

"If the two of you have indulged enough in personalities for the time being," Uncle Bert said in a tone of distaste, "I suggest that we get back to the problem at hand. Why didn't Mary Ann's seducer marry her? The obvious thing would be to assume that she would inherit the Rutherford fortune."

Delightful as he is, Uncle Bert occasionally has an air of insufferable superiority that is hard to bear. His very understatement was a kind of reproof that brought heightened color to Forrest's face. I doubt if he often got a taste of his own medicine.

"Rutherford would not have turned over a single penny under duress," he said. "And he'd have broken the man before the fellow even knew what was happening to him."

"As he is trying to break Jimmy," I said, going back to the one thing of importance to me, and I gave Forrest a brief résumé of the disasters that had struck Jimmy since Mary Ann's suicide, concluding with the early morning mugging.

"I hesitate to introduce any logic into this discussion," Uncle Bert said, "but let us stick to the point. How many people would be in a position to know how Mr. Rutherford would react to his daughter's marriage? The accounts I saw in the British press all spoke of her as heiress to a great fortune.

Who was likely to know what would happen to the man who married the girl without her father's approval?"

Forrest was silent, brooding about the question. Then he shook his head. "Aside from myself, I don't know of any man who would be in a position to assess the situation correctly. What baffles me is how Mary Ann was able to meet either your brother or any other man, assuming there was another man." Seeing my expression, he hurried on, "After all, she was never left alone."

"But why wasn't she?" I demanded. "It isn't just because she wasn't quite bright and needed protection. Mrs. Rutherford has been treated the same way ever since I met her. She is spied on every minute. What is Mr. Rutherford afraid that either of them could do? Because he was afraid and he is afraid now."

"Which brings us," Uncle Bert said, "to the factor of blackmail. I assume you have some basis for believing that it is going on."

Forrest nodded. "Oh, yes. I know he is paying blackmail. I don't know why. I don't know to whom. I don't know how much. I feel as though I were shadowboxing."

"I take it he hasn't informed the police."

"So far as I can make out, he thinks if he can get his hands on the guy he can silence him effectively."

"You appear to take a somewhat detached view of murder," commented Uncle Bert.

Forrest shrugged. "I wouldn't let it come to that."

Uncle Bert gave him a sharp, scrutinizing glance and I could understand his perplexity. Forrest was apparently the well-trained subordinate of a powerful man. But anything less subordinate than his attitude would be difficult to imagine. He sat in his usual easy posture, tall and thin and very elegant in his beautifully tailored suit, seeming about as aggressive as the lilies in the field, and yet he spoke casually of "not letting it come to that," as though he were not only master of his fate but of Rutherford's.

"No man on God's green earth should be trusted with the kind of power Rutherford wields. And he is vulnerable. He has to be vulnerable. He's got a weak spot. It stands to reason that there is something in his background he is scared as hell of having brought out into the open."

"And you assume that someone has discovered what it is and is putting on pressure," Uncle Bert said.

"Oh, I'm sure of it but there is not a damned thing that would stand up in a court of law."

"And that's where you want him to stand?"

"That's where I want him to stand."

There was a pause that Uncle Bert made no attempt to break. At length Forrest grinned ruefully. "I've said so much already I might as well give you the whole story. I fell asleep one afternoon in Rutherford's study. I'd been working a double shift on something else and cutting my sleep down to three hours. There's a big high-backed chair drawn up to the fireplace and that was my undoing. I intended to catch a few minutes of sleep and I dropped off as though I'd been slugged.

"Rutherford must have come in quietly. I didn't hear him but I did hear him telephone. He said, 'Last time I told you that was it. Not another penny. You can do your damnedest.' And then there was a long time while the other man spoke. Rutherford said, 'Okay, five thousand mailed the usual way . . . What name? . . . But get this straight. No man can bleed me and get away with it.' Then he banged down the telephone. He opened his wall safe which is built into a hinged bookcase and pulled out a packet of bonds, chose one, put it in a long green envelope and addressed it. He went out to mail it himself."

"You seem to have uncovered a lot," Uncle Bert commented.

"Except what this guy knows or has that forces Rutherford to pay through the teeth. Bearer bonds. He had a whole stack of them."

"That's odd, you know," Uncle Bert said, "especially in a man who likes to see money breed. It would be interesting to know what he is up to, supplying himself with negotiable bonds."

"Well, for one thing," I put in, "I heard him tell Forrest your estate was bought by a colleague of his."

Uncle Bert gasped. "But it was an Arab oil man!"

"Exactly," I said, "and how do you think the government men would like that? And, another thing, he is afraid of something that his wife and daughter knew, something they might tell someone, something he believes Mary Ann told Jimmy — only Jimmy said she didn't. All he knows is that she hated her father, really hated him."

Uncle Bert abandoned any further attempt to deal with the mystery of Mary Ann. "And you can't make any guess as to why Rutherford is being blackmailed?"

Forrest shook his head. "I don't believe all the facilities of the Treasury could unscramble the man's affairs. At this stage I doubt if he could do it himself. He has taken over so many companies and created so many interlocking directorates that the thing has become a nightmare. And Rutherford isn't the trustful type. He doesn't know how to delegate authority. He doesn't let his right hand know what his left hand is doing. God knows what sort of tangle his affairs are in. So far he has kept clear of the law, but it can't go on. One day the whole thing is going to become so top-heavy that it will collapse completely. I've had a growing feeling, Lord Glydes, that he knows the collapse is just a matter of time. I have suspicions but no proof — so far."

Uncle Bert raised his brows slightly but made no comment.

"Rutherford is not the kind to leave no escape hatch, at least for himself. Come the clash and it will be his subordinates who will be buried in the debris. Meantime he has one burning ambition, the only one he has been unable to satisfy, and he is willing to gamble a lot to achieve it."

"I take it I am supposed to be an instrument in paving the way for him in London society," Uncle Bert said dryly.

"The suggestion was made," Forrest admitted, with an unloving look at me.

"I'm afraid that, for a man with so few illusions, Rutherford still retains some about English society. That much money, unfortunately, insures a man a certain welcome almost everywhere. Rutherford doesn't need my seal of approval. You have only to look at the guest lists of some of our more dubious financial wizards to see that they include everyone, from royalty down. There seems to be a special aura about money. You remember Somerset Maugham's tart comment that he could understand the way people hang on the words of the rich if only gold coins dropped from their mouths — or words to that effect."

Forrest glanced at his watch and indicated that it was time for him to leave.

"Tell Rutherford you've been lunching with me, and I suggested that you both join me for cocktails in a few days. I'll give you a ring."

Forrest grinned. "I detect in you the makings of a conspirator."

"I'm beginning to find it rather amusing; at least, I would if Jennifer were not involved. Now that her cover has been blown . . ."

"How is that?" Forrest asked in surprise.

I stared at him. "Didn't you steal my letter?"

His jaw dropped. "I beg your pardon!"

For the first time I saw his resemblance to the public library lions. Insufferable. "The letter I wrote to Philip Hanning and hid under the blotter on the desk in my sitting room."

"Outside of my duties," Forrest said, and at his tone Uncle Bert looked at him alertly, "I'm not good at keyhole work."

"Well, someone took it. I thought that was why you followed me here today."

"I don't like to seem discourteous, but you were not my — uh — quarry. I was never more surprised than when I found you lunching with Lord Glydes. He was the one I was after. What was in this letter?"

I told him.

"So someone knows you are checking on Dr. Reynolds and that you are afraid for Mrs. Rutherford. The reference to Uncle Bert and the camel might be confusing. How did you sign it?"

"Jennifer," I said meekly.

Forrest opened his mouth, then closed it again.

All of a sudden I exclaimed, "Max!"

Forrest blinked.

"Max the chauffeur. He could easily meet Mary Ann and he's the best-looking man I've ever seen — and simply loaded with sex appeal, which he knows perfectly well."

"Max." Forrest considered the possibility. "It could be. He'd have the opportunity and, according to you, he has the necessary qualifications." His tone was not flattering to my judgment.

Uncle Bert looked at him, looked away.

"He would know that Rutherford would never consent to a marriage between him and Mary Ann," Forrest said, "though perhaps he thought if she were pregnant . . . No, I doubt it. Rutherford would handle that. But if Mary Ann were to have confided in Max something she knew or overheard, probably without even understanding it, he'd have fruitful material for blackmail, though he'd be taking the hell of a chance. Personally I wouldn't care to tangle with Rutherford."

"Now that's odd," Uncle Bert said. "I had gathered that you wouldn't hesitate a moment if it came down to basics."

Forrest made no response to this unexpected encomium. "But as I didn't purloin the letter — and I assume you looked carefully — someone else has it. And that is not so good if it should be Max."

"Does he have the run of the Rutherford apartment?" Uncle Bert asked in some surprise.

"No, but he has every female employee in the place dithering over him and seeking his approval. Any one of them would carry out any order he gave them without hesitation. I agree with you, Lord Glydes, that Jennifer had better not return to the apartment."

"Just the same," I insisted, "if we could prove that Max is the one behind the black-mail, Rutherford would have to call off the dogs and let Jimmy alone, wouldn't he? And he may have the key to the very evidence you are trying to establish."

"But we don't actually know that Max had anything to do with it," Forrest pointed out. "Anyhow it is absurd for you to go on with this masquerade."

"Absurd or not, that's what I intend to do until Rutherford removes me forcibly. Uncle Bert, will you explain to Jimmy and Philip so they won't worry about me? Jimmy is tripped on my having masculine protection."

Uncle Bert's brows arched in astonishment. "I had assumed that Preston here would keep an eye on you — unless, that is, I have mistaken my man, and I'm supposed to be a good judge of men and horseflesh. Now if you two will run along, I'd like to get forty winks. God, how I hate growing old!"

# 9

As we strolled up Fifth Avenue to the apartment, after leaving Uncle Bert, Forrest said, "He's quite a guy."

I gave him a brief sketch of the Glydes family and explained Uncle Cliffe's relationship with them.

"Radcliffe Bartlett! So he's your uncle. With all that money and influence I don't see why you and your brother need bother with a little antiques shop. Not," he added hastily, "that there is anything wrong with an antiques shop."

"Now that's big of you," I said.

Forrest grinned. "Oh, come off it, Jennifer! That's not a chip you've got on your shoulder, it's a whole log and practically toppling. Just asking to be knocked off."

I smoldered in silence, until a sidelong glance revealed an amused half-smile on his lips. I laughed. "Well, for one thing, we like being independent. And for another, Jimmy loves the antiques business. And anyhow —"

"Anyhow, it is no concern of mine," Forrest admitted. "But what does concern me is the effect of Lord Glydes knowing that the Arab oil man who bought Glydes Park is a colleague of the next ambassador to Great Britain. It opens up potentials."

"Are you so married to Mr. Rutherford's interests?"

"Well, let's say I am concerned in them. We'd better leave it at that for the time being. And that reminds me, Jennifer, you'd be wise not to let the man know how much of his dubious activities you have been able to put together."

"Well, if he has seen my letter, he already knows that I am not Mary Ann Weldone and that I didn't get that job in order to be a companion."

"What would interest me most," Forrest said, "would be to discover that he never saw that letter. I have a growing feeling that there is a very skillful operator at work somewhere."

"What's your real job?"

"I'll tell you some day. Not now. And why those dark glasses you have been wearing?"

"My eyes and brows are just like Jimmy's, and Mr. Rutherford has seen Jimmy so he'd be bound to notice the resemblance. People always do."

"Oh, in that case I suppose you had better

put them on again, though it is a pity."

I did so, aware that while it was no extravagant compliment it was better than nothing. Anyhow, who wants fulsome compliments? We walked on in silence.

At last he said, "I can't grasp what you can do at the Rutherford apartment that I can't do better." Seeing the storm gather, he amended his words. "I mean in the way of uncovering a blackmailer." He added plaintively, "You are as prickly as a cactus. Honestly, you'd do better just to clear off and leave it to me."

"And what happens to Mrs. Rutherford?"

"Well, what happened to her this morning?" he pointed out reasonably. "Dr. Reynolds took charge and there wasn't a damned thing you could do about it."

"And if he puts that poor woman in some sort of institution — what then?"

"I'll have someone check on the good doctor and find out what kind of professional standing he has — and whether he had Mary Ann as a patient about six or eight months ago. But that will take time. Getting any reliable information about a patient is never easy."

"And with Rutherford in such a hurry to get his wife out of the way," I pointed out, "time is the one thing we don't have."

"I know that." Forrest touched my arm and steered me across the street at a light, and we went more slowly past the big apartment buildings. "And probably for you there's no more time at all."

I was startled. "What do you mean?"

"Simply that if Rutherford succeeds in shutting his wife away, temporarily at any rate, there would be no job for you." After a moment, as I digested this, he asked, "What would you do if Rutherford fired you?"

"I don't know," I said blankly. "Go back to the shop, I suppose. Someone ought to be there to keep the business from going to wrack and ruin. According to Jimmy, it is in a bad way already because of Rutherford's tactics."

"I don't like it. You might not be safe there. What about this man you were discussing with your brother over the telephone?"

"Philip Hanning, you mean? No, that's out. I can't go on letting Philip do things for me unless —"

Forrest bumped into a woman on the sidewalk and apologized. "Sorry, I wasn't paying attention." He turned to me. "From what I saw of him the day I checked on that reference" — and he grinned — "he seems to be a nice guy. He certainly gave you a glowing send-off."

"He is nice — the best friend either Jimmy or I has ever had. But he is not included in my future plans." It occurred to me that there was no reason for trying to make this point clear to Forrest.

"He's well heeled, on top of his job, devoted to your interests. What does a girl want these days?"

That required no answer. We were nearly at our destination and we had automatically slowed down. From now on we would have little opportunity for private conversation.

"I have been thinking of that missing letter of yours, Jennifer," Forrest said. "If one of the maids took it from your desk and gave it to Max, you could be in a lot of trouble. That is, assuming — as you seem to have done — that he is the one who is blackmailing Rutherford. I haven't had any dealings with him myself beyond knowing he is a competent driver, and he seems to be a loyal henchman of Rutherford's. I don't know where he lives; I don't know his background, whether he is married or where Rutherford dug him up. I don't even know his last name — yes I do though. Baker. I saw it on a cancelled check of Rutherford's when I was going over some stuff for him. It just didn't connect until now. I'll put a man onto checking Max."

*Put a man.* That sounded as though Forrest had a sizable staff to draw on for his
purpose, and his manner of taking this for
granted added to its effectiveness. I stole a
look at him. Obviously he had obtained
Uncle Bert's seal of approval, which was not
accorded lightly. In his unstressed way,
Uncle Bert took certain values seriously.

"Meanwhile," Forrest went on, "watch
out for him, Jennifer. And if you have an opportunity, you might look over the female
members of the staff and see who is doing
Max's snooping for him — if, of course,
anyone is, and we aren't piling suspicion on
the guy without justification."

"A man like that just plain arouses suspicion," I said.

At the corner Forrest halted. "I suggest
that it would be the better part of valor if
you were to go in alone. I'll hang around and
come back in a quarter of an hour. No use
giving people any ideas." His hand closed
over my arm. "Watch yourself, Jennifer. I'll
try to keep an eye on you, but I don't have a
lot of free time. Rutherford himself keeps
me hopping, aside —"

"Aside from your real job, whatever it is."

He gave me an exasperated glance and
then shrugged. "Too true. And bear this in
mind. I'm all for chivalry and the marines to

the rescue. But in this case I have a job that takes priority even over your safety. It has to come first. I'm committed. That's why I wish to God you'd go away somewhere."

## II

The usual maid opened the door for me. "Mrs. Rutherford was asking for you, Miss Weldone."

"When?"

"Just after Dr. Reynolds left. Perhaps eleven-thirty."

"I'll go to her at once."

"She is resting now, and the doctor left orders that she was not to be disturbed."

I went up to my rooms on the third floor without seeing anyone. The bedroom door was open and someone moved a dresser drawer closed softly. From the doorway I could see Rose Miller, Mrs. Rutherford's stout secretary, lifting a pile of slips, feeling under them. Of course! Why hadn't I thought of her? She had run after me when I left the apartment; she had tried to find out "what had really happened." She had told me to leave the mail for Max. Because she was older and unattractive, I had automatically dropped her from my calculations. But if Max were half as astute as I believed him to be, the woman would be a natural. Unmarried, and presumably unsought, she'd fall into his hands without a struggle, a born victim. If my own safety and Jimmy's and Mrs. Rutherford's hadn't been at stake, I'd have felt sorry for her.

Instead, I stood in the bedroom doorway and said, "Well!" in a tone of outraged surprise.

She whirled around, her eyes behind bifocals staring at me, mouth open. No one ever looked more guilty when caught in the act. In her haste and confusion she tried to slam the drawer shut and caught a finger in it. She gave a sharp cry of pain.

I was tempted to say, "There's nothing in there to interest Max. You're wasting your time," but I refrained.

"I was looking —" she began, and broke off.

"So I see." I added with a cruelty I didn't know I was capable of, "I don't keep any money in bureau drawers, and don't own any jewelry."

She flushed an ugly mottled color. "I was only . . ." she began.

Somewhat to my own surprise I took pity on her. "It's all right. I didn't need more than a day to see the situation here. I suppose Mr. Rutherford forced you to spy on other members of the household."

She was slow to recognize the lifeline I had thrown her. "Yes, it was Mr. Rutherford," she said in relief. "Men like that, you know, with so terribly much money and everyone after it, have to take more precautions than other people."

I nodded and stood waiting for her to leave. She didn't know how to handle the situation. Her face was still flushed, and she stood rubbing the finger she had bruised in the dresser drawer.

"Well, I — this is my free time, as Mrs. Rutherford usually rests for a good part of the afternoon, and today, of course, she is under doctor's orders. I'm going out for a while. Taking the car. Mrs. Rutherford is always so generous about that! If there is anything I can do for you, an errand . . ."

"Nothing, thank you."

I watched her go and knew that she was hastening off to report to Max. Only after she had gone did I wonder belatedly whether I had blundered in letting her know that I had found her searching my possessions. Well, it was too late to retrieve my mistake — if it had been a mistake.

The apartment seemed very quiet. On this floor there was otherwise only the secretary's bedroom and office and some unoccupied guest rooms. The staff — with the exception of Max, who lived out — had their rooms on another floor of the building.

I hung up my fur coat carefully and saw the two new evening dresses, which I had not yet worn, on scented hangers. One was green velvet and the other a soft, sheer material with silver threads shining in it. I was examining them in delight when I heard the faint scratching on the sitting-room door and went to admit Mrs. Rutherford. She came in and closed the door soundlessly behind her. I took one look at her face. With an exclamation of concern, I pushed her gently into a chair and knelt beside her, taking her ice-cold hands in mine.

"What's wrong?" I asked. "What's wrong?"

For a moment she was rigid, and then she relaxed and began to shake.

"Let me get you something. Shall I call Hilda?"

"No, she is a nice girl, but there is nothing she can do for me."

"I want to help you, but I don't know how."

"Just by being here, by being yourself, Mary Ann."

I tightened my grip on her hands and

made her look at me. "Mrs. Rutherford," I spoke slowly and distinctly, "I want to make you understand that I am myself. I am not your daughter."

Her eyes evaded mine, then came back, pleading, frightened, imploring. I made her look at me. "It would be easier," I said as gently as I could, "to let her go."

"I can't! I can't!"

"Everyone has to do it some time or other. We can't escape death."

"But not Mary Ann. She is alive. She has to be."

"Why?"

"Because" — and her lips shook, her voice was out of control — "if she is not alive, I killed her."

"That's horrible and it's not true."

"It is true. Oh God, it is true! If she died it is because of the sleeping pills — my sleeping pills. They are gone, the ones I collected for months — months. I wanted to be dead. But not Mary Ann. Never Mary Ann. I just couldn't go on living with Paul. He let Dr. Reynolds shut up Mary Ann, not only to get her out of the way, but to make clear to me that she was a sort of hostage, a way of insuring my good behavior, my obedience." The word was bitter on her lips because she was, or at least she had been, a proud woman.

"I should have thrown the pills away when I knew I didn't have the courage to use them, as I threw away the medicine Dr. Reynolds left me this morning."

As I started to withdraw my hands she grasped them, holding me down on my knees. "Mary Ann."

"I am not your daughter." I had captured her eyes and her attention again. "Please listen to me, Mrs. Rutherford. You are not to blame for your daughter's suicide. She had a problem to solve that she couldn't handle and she chose that way. She just went to sleep. It is hard to accept, in a way, but you must believe me when I tell you that you are not to blame. If she had not found that easy way, she would have had to choose a harder one."

I let her think about that for a moment, shifting my position slightly because my foot had gone to sleep and my legs were cramped from my awkward position, kneeling beside her.

"Life hasn't been very fair to Mary Ann, has it?" I said gently.

"The papers always called her 'the girl who had everything,' " her mother said.

"Except an adult mind. She would have found life more difficult as she grew older without growing up — much more difficult.

What can be overlooked in a young and pretty girl is only an irritant in a middle-aged woman. Mary Ann needed to be taken care of, and yet she wasn't happy when she was surrounded by all this luxury and she couldn't learn to live without it. She was a victim. Try to think of her as resting now, with all her problems behind her."

What seemed like hours and must have been at least half an hour dragged by before Mrs. Rutherford's grip on my hands relaxed. I got slowly to my feet. She drew a long shuddering breath. "You are sure I am not to blame for Mary Ann's death?"

"Positive."

She did not ask how I knew, seeming to assume omniscience on my part. She pulled herself out of the chair and stood swaying for a moment; then she straightened up. "If you would stand by, I think I could learn how to manage without seeking ways to run away from life and from myself." And then her color drained away. "I was forgetting! You won't be here to help me."

"You mean I'm being fired?"

"Not exactly. Paul wants you to have a nice check, but, of course, when I go away, there will be nothing for you to do here."

"You are going away?"

She nodded. "Tomorrow. Dr. Reynolds"

157

— she moistened her lips — "is taking me to his sanitarium in Westchester for a while until I get over the shock of Mary Ann's death. He and Paul think that will be best for me."

"Mrs. Rutherford," I said quickly, "you are forgetting what I told you. You aren't to blame for your daughter's death. You have faced the truth and you are free now. You don't need a rest cure. There's no reason for you to be sent away."

"Paul has decided," she said flatly. "Dr. Reynolds left me some medicine to take — but I didn't. I washed it down the toilet. I knew what it was. It was to keep me quiet until he can have me removed to the sanitarium, that horrible place where Mary Ann went last spring after she overheard the conversation her father had recorded with —" She put her hand over her mouth and stared at me.

"You don't have to go anywhere you don't choose to," I told her.

She laughed without mirth. "You don't know Paul. I was useful to him when we were married, because my family had a certain social position, which he needed. We weren't rich but we were respected. Isn't it queer how many people choose to live outside the law and yet long for respectability?

Not the thing itself but the appearance of it. Gangsters who want their children to go to the best schools. Not for an education but for a kind of status. Paul's people, from all I can make out, were petty gangsters, and he was impressed by my people."

The flood of reminiscence broke off and then went on again. "But I'm not important to him now. Not anymore. Not with the things I know. Not with his plans for the future, which don't include me. I know that. Paul wants me dead, as he wanted Mary Ann dead. He is afraid of what I might say about the tape."

"What tape?"

"Mary Ann found it when she was looking for some rock music. It was in with a stack of tapes but it wasn't music. It was a conversation about transferring large blocks of money to Swiss bank accounts in order to escape taxation. He's dishonest, you know. Paul has always been dishonest, but I would never have betrayed him because I was brought up to fear scandal. Mary Ann wouldn't have either, because she didn't understand what it meant. All that she ever knew was that when she spoke about the tape, which she had mistaken for rock music, she thought it was funny. Instead, Paul was furious and he terrified her."

"So that's what he was afraid of," I said slowly. "Where is the tape now, do you know?"

She shook her head. "I have no idea." It was obvious, too, that she had no idea of the significance of the importance of that tape.

"With whom did your husband have that conversation he recorded?"

Mrs. Rutherford shook her head. "I promised never to tell. Never."

I wondered if Max had the tape or whether, at least, he had learned of its existence from Mary Ann. If that was the case, he'd have set Rose Miller on its track. If, that is, the thing had disappeared and was not still in Rutherford's possession. If he had lost it, he would pay heavily to get it back. Once it was known that he was defrauding the government on his taxes, he would be in bad trouble. Instead of an ambassadorship he would have a long prison term and his financial kingdom would topple.

Mrs. Rutherford shivered. "Once I enter that sanitarium . . ."

"Well," I said matter-of-factly, "you aren't going to enter that sanitarium."

"What could you do to prevent it — to stop Paul and Dr. Reynolds?" There was no hope in her. Whatever diminishing hope had survived the years had dwindled to ash with Mary Ann's suicide. But there must be some faint spark while there was breath in her, and I had to fan it to life.

# 10

"Are all the telephones in this apartment on one line?" I asked.

Mrs. Rutherford shook her head. "No, Paul has a private wire in his bedroom and another in his study." As I got up she asked sharply, "What are you going to do?"

"Arrange a place where you will be safe, at least for tonight."

"I'd never get out of here, and there's no place where Paul couldn't find me — Paul or Max or Forrest."

"Not Forrest," I said. "You can count on him."

It dawned on me that I had no reason to believe Forrest would lift a hand for her. He had, as he had made painfully clear, other irons in the fire, and her safety did not concern him. Well, he wasn't the only possibility.

"What are the immediate plans?"

With the first stirring of hope, Mrs. Rutherford pulled herself together. "I was to be doped most of today and tonight; in the morning Dr. Reynolds is to call for me and take me to the sanitarium. Meanwhile I am not supposed to see anyone."

"What about Hilda?"

"Oh, she is to be dismissed, too. Of course, there won't be anything for her to do here, with me in a sanitarium, and Paul does not intend me to come back. I'm sorry for her. She needs the money in order to get married, and I think she is really fond of me and loyal, and she doesn't like the way things are done here."

"I'm with her there!"

Mrs. Rutherford glanced nervously around her.

"You make me think of someone under Communist control," I burst out furiously, "afraid to have anyone hear what is said. This is your own apartment, isn't it?"

"Do you think so?" There was quiet irony in her speech.

"All right, we'll make our first dash for freedom, take our first gamble. I'm going to call Hilda and ask her to come up here."

In a few minutes a tap at the door announced Hilda, who, as she came in, glanced at Mrs. Rutherford in surprise. "Is Madam all right? I thought she was lying down."

"Thought I'd be unconscious after all that dope?" Mrs. Rutherford asked, and Hilda, looking startled, nodded.

"Look here, Hilda," I said, taking matters into my own hands, "you know, don't you, that Mrs. Rutherford is supposed to go into a sanitarium tomorrow?"

She nodded.

This was the sticky part. "She doesn't want to go, Hilda. I've got an idea that I could get her away for a while, but I'd need some help."

"There'd be a great scandal," Hilda pointed out.

"There couldn't be. Whatever happened, Mr. Rutherford wants no publicity. What I need is someone to help me get her out of this building without notice."

"I'd help Madam if I could, but there's a doorman and a guard downstairs. She just couldn't walk out unnoticed."

"Yes, she could, if she wore my fur coat and dark glasses. She's about my size. Oh, she'd have to have something over her head."

Hilda thought about it. "There's Madam's secretary. She is always barging in."

"Stop making difficulties. Tell her the doctor said she was to see no one. Actually, she already knows that. She told me so. She won't be a trouble to you."

"And there's Max."

At her tone I grinned. "I take it you haven't fallen for Max."

Hilda flushed. "I'm engaged to be married and I've told him so, but for all the difference that would make to him — so I had to say if he ever tried to so much as kiss me again my Jack would tear him apart. And he could, too. Light heavyweight boxer."

I laughed. "Now that's the kind of man to have on our side!"

"But if Madam gets away, Mr. Rutherford will know I must be in on it, and I don't want to have any trouble. Jack wouldn't like it. We are going to be married in six months when we've saved enough money, and any scandal could hurt his popularity with his fans."

"You're to be fired anyhow," I said brutally. "You haven't anything to lose."

"I have my own checking account," Mrs. Rutherford said, hope having given her a little courage, a little initiative. "I could arrange for you to have enough money to get married now."

"Jack wouldn't like me to take money I hadn't earned."

"More power to Jack, but you will earn it," I assured her.

"Would six months' salary be all right?"

Mrs. Rutherford asked.

Hilda's expression was enough.

"Suppose I make out a check now and you can cash it before the bank closes. Then when you get back we can plan what I am to take with me." Mrs. Rutherford's faith in me, her assumption that I could provide a safe haven, shook me.

"If you are supposed to go to a sanitarium in the morning, I'll probably get my notice to quit tonight. Then your escape in my outfit would be a natural, and you could take my suitcases."

"But what about you?"

"I'll figure out something. Don't worry about that."

While Mrs. Rutherford went back to her own suite to plan what she should take with her, I went down to her husband's study. I was stopped at the door by the sound of Forrest's voice, but as it went on and on I realized that he must be using the dictating machine.

I pushed open the door cautiously and looked in. Without turning around, Forrest said, "What is it, Jennifer? I thought we weren't to be seen together."

"How did you know who I was?" I was startled.

"Saw you reflected in that picture. Better

come in. Don't hover."

"A lot has been happening." I told him about the tape with its revelation that Rutherford was transferring large amounts of money to numbered accounts in Switzerland. It was the accidental discovery of the tape that had led to Mary Ann's incarceration in the sanitarium. And now, unless she had help, Mrs. Rutherford was to be taken there in the morning. I also sketched in the reason for Mrs. Rutherford's inability to accept the fact of her daughter's death. The words tumbled over each other in my haste to explain the situation before we were interrupted.

"So that's where Mary Ann got the sleeping pills!" Forrest exclaimed. "That clears up one mystery." He gave me an odd look and shook his head. "I've spent seven months trying to get some of the information you've picked up in a few hours. And where do you plan to send Mrs. Rutherford?"

"To Philip Hanning's house. She would be safe there."

"Is your friend Hanning willing to run a port of missing persons?"

By way of answer I picked up the telephone and called Philip's office and explained the situation. "She's got to get away today, Philip. Once she is in that sanitarium, committed by her own husband, it would take a miracle to get her out. . . . Oh, I have a plan to get her away from the apartment. She'll wear my clothes and dark glasses. . . . I don't know. I'll figure out something for myself. . . .

"Of course I'll be all right. . . . Come up to your house, too? I think I'd better go back to the shop and send Jenks up to you. With two Rutherford refugees under your roof, you'll need another man about the place, because I assume Jimmy isn't capable of putting up much of a fight yet — if it should come to that. . . .

"Nonsense, there's nothing to worry about. . . . All right, I promise I'll call you as soon as I get to the shop. Oh, no, I can't. The phones may be tapped. Well, I'll find a drugstore or call you in the morning. . . . All right, tonight then. . . . Philip, I am truly grateful. I knew you wouldn't fail me."

"I suppose you realize," Forrest said when I had put down the telephone, "that this escapade of yours is all that is needed to support Rutherford's claim that his wife is unhinged."

"Well, if he can't put hands on her it won't matter."

"God help you if that is what you think," Forrest said.

# II

If I hadn't been prepared, I would have accepted without hesitation Mr. Rutherford's bland explanation of his wife's condition and the decision to have her rest for a while under Dr. Reynolds' care in his Westchester sanitarium.

"As my poor Sarah will not require your services for some time to come, I have prepared a check for a month's salary in lieu of notice. And if you will leave an address, we will get in touch with you as soon as she returns here, as she appears to be so fond of you, Miss Weldone. She asked me to tell you how sorry she is not to be able to say goodbye personally, but she was sure you would understand."

Rutherford was sitting behind the impressive desk in his study where I had talked to Forrest a few hours earlier. He handed me a check for $750 and added briskly, "Now if you will let me have an address where I can reach you. . . ."

"Well, I haven't any address. Perhaps the room I was renting before I came to Mrs. Rutherford is still vacant. I can inquire tomorrow."

"The thing is that it might be advisable for you to leave tonight. Now, in fact, Max will take you wherever you'd care to go, and if you require cash for a night's lodging I'd be happy to advance it." He pulled out a billfold and handed me two twenties and a ten-dollar bill. He was certainly hellbent on getting me out of the place, which, of course, was just what I wanted. But one thing emerged as clear as crystal. He had not seen the missing letter, which had to mean that it was in Max's possession.

The situation was perfect for me and could not have fitted better into the plans that had already been made. I tried hard not to look as pleased as I felt and agreed that I could be ready to leave in half an hour.

Rutherford smiled. "Max will be waiting for you," he said and held out his hand. "Sorry it has been such a brief visit, Miss Weldone."

I murmured something and escaped up the stairs to Mrs. Rutherford's rooms, where I explained that everything was all set. She was to be on her way in half an hour. Max would be waiting for her with the car, assuming I was to be his passenger.

"You won't even have to speak," I assured her when I saw her alarm at having to face Max. "Hilda will go down with you, carrying one of my suitcases, and she can say, 'Where do you want to go? the Waldorf?'

That would be best because there are so many ways out of the place. Then when Max has left you, take a cab to Philip Hanning's house, where you are expected and you will be safe." I gave her the address and telephone number.

I had not warned her that she was going to encounter her son-in-law as another guest. I'd have to leave that to Philip's ingenuity. Anyhow she couldn't help liking Jimmy.

After a last encouraging word and a hug, I left Mrs. Rutherford and went up to my own rooms, carrying the bandbox Hilda had unearthed for me and into which I packed my clothes. There was no room for the three beautiful evening dresses and I left them behind with regret, knowing I'd never have anything so lovely again. The door to Rose Miller's bedroom was ajar, and I could hear her singing softly to herself. Evidently Max had rewarded her adequately for her information that afternoon.

I waited then, picturing what was happening: Mrs. Rutherford, wearing my coat and dark glasses, was going down the stairs, carrying one of my suitcases, while Hilda went along, carrying the other. They would take the elevator to the big lobby, where they would have to pass the doorman and the guard. Both undoubtedly knew that the

171

companion had lost her job, so they would be expecting her. I hoped to God that she would not collapse until she had reached a safe harbor, but I wouldn't have placed any money on it. Twenty-odd years of Rutherford would erode Superman's self-confidence. How much, I wondered, had her family had to do with that wholly incompatible marriage. I wouldn't put it beyond the man to have bought her, openly and cynically, for the prestige of her background, that intangible advantage he could not acquire in any other way. I was grateful for Uncle Cliffe and Jimmy and my imperfectly remembered parents, who had not worshipped Mammon.

I finished packing, moving quietly because I did not want to attract attention from Rose Miller, who would assume that I had already left. Then I switched off the lights and stole down the stairs to Mrs. Rutherford's suite, where Hilda was waiting for me, her eyes bright with excitement.

"Did she get away all right?"

Hilda nodded. "It worked like a charm. And she seemed — oh, confident, you know. You've done a lot for her, Miss Weldone. Now about you. Here's an old winter coat of mine. It's too big for you, but better than nothing. We'll do down through the delivery entrance. The only problem is that we'll have to go through the kitchen. I'll go first and get the chef out of the way for a couple of minutes."

"Sure you can manage?"

She laughed mischievously. "He is always making passes. I'll tell him I was fired and pour out my troubles. You just slip through and out the door. The freight elevator is right outside. Wait for me on the ground floor."

The worst part was reaching the kitchen without being seen. Fortunately no one was yet setting the dining room table and the butler's pantry was deserted. I heard Hilda's voice as she spoke to the chef, and then the voices faded as they withdrew into another room. I sped through the kitchen, out the door, closing it quietly behind me, and rang the bell for the freight elevator.

It seemed to me that the thing crawled up to the twelfth floor, and at any moment I expected someone to stop me. But at last it came, a vast elevator equipped to carry heavy furniture, and began the slow journey down. On the main floor I went to stare out at the side street, looking at the row of private houses, at the trees in their small plots of ground, and thinking how secure the people must be, until I remembered that security was the one thing the Rutherford apartment did not provide.

Then the elevator door opened and Hilda joined me, carrying a battered old suitcase. "I told you," she said triumphantly. "Well, I guess this is good-bye, Miss Weldone."

"Are you going to be all right, Hilda?"

She nodded. "I telephoned while I was out. I am going to stay with Jack's sister until we are married, in a few days, now that I've got that check. All I wish is that I could know what happens to Mrs. Rutherford."

"If you tell me how to reach you, I'll let you know."

"Thanks. And I'd sleep a lot better if I knew you were all right, Miss Weldone." She gave me a telephone number and then added, half laughing, half embarrassed, "If there's any problem, just call. Jack is a good man in time of trouble." Then she waved her hand and went quickly down the street toward Madison Avenue, carrying her suitcase.

# 11

The whole operation had worked out so smoothly that I was in a state of euphoria when I climbed on a Fifth Avenue bus and headed downtown for the shop. Mrs. Rutherford was probably safe in Philip's house by now. Hilda would soon be with her fiancé, who appeared to be more than capable of looking after her. And I was free of Rutherford, though I had lost my opportunity to uncover the threat against Jimmy.

I found myself wondering what Forrest would think when Rutherford informed him over cocktails that I was already out of the house. Well, at least he knew that he could reach me through Uncle Bert. I didn't ask myself why this should be important.

Vaguely I was conscious of the lights from the great apartment buildings on Fifty-ninth Street and of the glow in the night sky from Broadway to the west. The bus stopped to pick up passengers and lumbered slowly down the avenue. Dimly I became aware of the voices of the two women behind me.

"Think of having that driver," the other

replied fervently, and they both laughed.

I turned my head and saw, keeping pace with the bus, a long Lincoln — and at the wheel a uniformed chauffeur wearing a peaked cap. I'd have known that profile anywhere.

I had a moment of complete panic and then tried to convince myself that Max's presence was sheer coincidence. He couldn't possibly have followed me. But I didn't believe it. I couldn't go back to the apartment; I was afraid to go on to the shop, which would make clear, if nothing else did, my association with Jimmy Bartlett.

The truly terrifying thing was that Max had found me, but that he had discovered the imposture and that Mrs. Rutherford was no longer safe, as I had assumed. Perhaps he had not left her at the Waldorf but had driven her off somewhere else. When the bus pulled in to the curb I got down. Before I could cross the street, the Lincoln had drawn up beside me and Max leaned back to open the door.

I managed to look surprised and then I shook my head. "Thanks very much but I don't need a lift," I called.

The arrogant eyes surveyed me with surprise, and then I remembered that he had never seen me without the concealing and disfiguring glasses.

"Well," he said on a long-drawn-out note of approval that was probably designed to flutter my heart but that made me yearn for Hilda's prizefighter. I'd have given a lot to see that self-confident smirk wiped off his handsome mouth. Then the smirk faded. "Get in," he said, and this time it was an order.

"I said no and I meant no."

"Women don't say no to me," he said softly, and I laughed.

"You make me think of a man like you — an actor named Lou Tellegan. He wrote a book that he called *Women Have Been Kind*, but the reviewers called it *Women Have Been Kind of Dumb* by Lou Kiss and Tellegan."

He didn't like that. He didn't like it at all. His expression changed, and for the first time I was afraid of him, afraid as I had not been of Rutherford, who had seemed much the more potentially dangerous.

"Get in," he said. "This is no time to be cute. I'm not playing. Get in or I'll follow you all over New York if necessary."

"What do you want of me?"

"Personally I don't want any part of you."

"That's mutual."

And then, so swiftly that I was not prepared, he slid out of the driver's seat and tossed me, literally tossed me, onto the floor of the car and threw the hatbox on top of me. Before I could disentangle myself and sit up, the car was moving again. Slowly I pulled myself onto the seat and saw that Max was watching me in the rearview mirror.

"Don't try any tricks," he warned me as my hand reached for the door release. "You'll break your neck if you try to jump."

I didn't try. I'd lost my chance to clear Jimmy through Mr. Rutherford but I might be able to bargain with Max. That he was spying on his employer through the secretary I knew. That he had read — and withheld — my letter I was convinced. And he couldn't do me any harm. Or could he?

"What was the idea of that game at the Waldorf, and why did you go back to the apartment?"

My heart leaped exultantly and I was weak with relief. He still assumed that it was I whom he had driven from the apartment. Sooner or later he would learn that he had been tricked, but I hoped it would be later. And meanwhile Mrs. Rutherford was safe! I nearly laughed out loud.

I had not followed the twisting and turning of the car, but as he slowed up I saw a street sign. We were on Third Avenue in the

Seventies. And then the car turned, went down a steep incline into an underground garage, and slid smoothly into a slot bearing the Lincoln's license number.

When he had shut off the motor, Max came around to take the hatbox and then to pull me out of the car, which he did with a brutal jerk that nearly threw me on my face. I knew then that this was part of a deliberate campaign to demoralize me through terror, which was a tactical error because it put me in a flaming temper that set the adrenalin flowing.

With my arm held in a bruising grip, he steered me across the sidewalk. There was no one in sight. A few cars were parked at the curb but they were unoccupied, and the evening was too cold for saunterers. We went into the narrow entrance to a walk-up apartment. Still holding my arm, he unlocked his mailbox, pulled out some letters, and then opened the inner door.

There was a blare of rock and roll music from the top floor. A blare? The ear was assaulted, deafened by the horrible din. The very air throbbed with the meaningless simple repeated phrases, the new savagery. On either side of the ground floor were darkened offices. Seeing my expression, Max smiled. "There's no one here in the evenings except on the top floor, a bunch of kids who like rock and roll and, I suspect, smoke grass. How else could they stand that uproar? They aren't interested in sounds coming from any other apartment."

There was a padlock outside the door on the second floor. He removed it and reached in to switch on lights. Then he stood back to let me get the full impact.

The room had a white carpet and white-satin upholstery on the furniture, white lamps and accessories. The most spectacular feature was a big chair upholstered in red velvet against a background of red velvet draperies that covered the windows and almost the whole front wall. And on a side wall, facing the door, was the Sisley!

The room, the product of an expensive decorator, was obviously Max's pride and delight. He waited to taste the full impact of it in my expression. So I laughed.

"Of all things! I would never have expected to find you living in such effeminate surroundings!" I laughed again.

It was the last reaction he could have anticipated and he was angry, so angry that the color drained out of his face and his breath came fast and hard. Then he said smoothly, "Really? Perhaps I can change your mind. What do you think, Jennifer?"

As he spoke my name I gave a convulsive start. Then I remembered that he did not necessarily know who I was. He was the man who had my letter, the letter which, for reasons of his own, he appeared not to have shown to Rutherford. This meant that he had a sideline of his own and therefore was vulnerable, if I could just find the weak spot.

Don't panic, I told myself. Don't panic. He won't gain anything by hurting you. (*Hurting* was a nice, euphemistic word.) Find out what he wants.

Well, it was a bit late to pretend to be overcome by his charm; I'd need something more convincing. He had dropped my arm now and I sat down, partly because my knees were so weak I was afraid to go on standing. One thing I knew. He was the thief who had stolen the real Sisley. Probably in his bedroom I'd find the Queen Carlotta dressing table, though I had no intention of looking that far.

Max settled himself in the red velvet chair with the air of Muhammad Ali saying, "I am the greatest," and I smothered the laughter that bubbled up in me. Max wasn't the stuff to stomach laughter at his expense.

"And now," he said, "we are going to talk about that letter you wrote."

So I had been right. Max had the letter. As

he had not mentioned it to Rutherford, he must be on a ploy of his own, which meant, didn't it, that he was probably the black-mailer. Of all the staff at Rutherford's establishment, he was the one with the most freedom of movement, with the exception, of course, of Forrest. Rose Miller was willing and eager to search the apartment or to do anything else he wanted. He was the one who could most easily have had secret meetings with poor Mary Ann, have seduced her — body and mind — with his pornography and his personal attractions. And through Mary Ann he could have learned of Rutherford's moving large sums of money out of the country and into Swiss bank accounts. It all fitted together.

If he knew I was not the girl I claimed to be, at least I knew of his activities. So far we were even. I could threaten to betray him to Rutherford, who would be a ruthless enemy. If Max was indeed the blackmailer, Rutherford was capable of murder to eliminate this threat from his path. One thing about really big money: it can buy life and death.

I waited, uncertain what to do. I didn't dare antagonize him too much, not while I was, in a sense, his prisoner.

"What's your interest in Mrs. Rutherford?" he asked abruptly.

"So it was to you that Rose Miller gave my letter." I sounded detached, a little amused. "I suppose you have to settle for the kind of silly elderly victim you can attract." And then I knew I had gone too far. The man's colossal vanity was like a hair trigger. Touch that and there would be an explosion. "Why didn't you show the letter to your boss?"

"That's my business. What about his wife?"

"I'm sorry for her. She's a tragic person and her husband seems to be trying to drive her permanently out of her mind. I don't want that to happen."

"I thought you'd never seen her until you met her at Tiffany's."

"I hadn't."

"Oh, come off it!"

"It's true. But it doesn't take long to know what is being done to her."

"So you got that job just to protect her?"

"No, I had a different reason for taking the job."

"And you aren't Mary Ann Weldone."

"No."

This admission took him by surprise. "Well, well. That's more like it. I thought you'd see reason. And who is Philip Hanning?"

I sat staring at him, realizing with a jolt that Mrs. Rutherford was now at Philip's and that Max had his address. How could I have been such a fool as to send her there? Somehow she had to be warned that she was no longer in a safe harbor, that I had let her down badly.

Max got out of his chair, walked in a leisurely way to mine, and then struck me across the cheek so violently that the blow snapped my head to one side, nearly dislocating my neck. I caught my breath, gasping, tears stinging my eyes.

"Next time I ask you a question, answer it." He went back to his chair. Judging by the way he sat, I thought the thing must symbolize a kind of throne. Like Rutherford, Max had a power complex.

Abruptly he switched his line of questioning. "Why did you go back to the apartment after I drove you to the Waldorf?"

"Uh . . ."

"When you left the second time, through the delivery entrance, Hilda was with you, wasn't she? I've always distrusted that girl."

"On the theory that if they don't fall for you they must be nuts?" If I could only learn to hold my tongue!

The hard eyes narrowed. His lower lip

pushed out over the upper. Then he re-peated, "Why did you go back?"

I didn't answer because I couldn't think of a convincing answer. Again Max approached me with that deliberate step. I cringed away from him, and again he struck me across the face, this time knocking my head in the opposite direction.

He stood over me. "Why did you go back?" He took my hand in his, almost gently, and then his thumb bored into the muscle between thumb and first finger. I gasped, moaned, and finally yelled. As he had said, the sound did not attract the noisy people on the floor above. I tugged at my hand. Again his thumb probed and again I yelled. I'm not the stuff heroes are made of.

"Why?"

And to my shame I cried out, "I didn't! I didn't!"

"But —" And then he stared at me. "Then she was — my God, it was Mrs. Rutherford making her getaway! And I drove her. The boss — the boss —" He choked. At the look he gave me I tried to push my way through the back of the chair. He was completely beside himself. He knocked my head from side to side; he slapped me with his open hand. His nostrils flared. I think it required all his self-restraint to keep his hands from my throat. He wanted to kill me, partly from fear of what might happen to him, partly in ungovernable rage at having been bested by a woman.

The telephone rang shrilly and he let my head fall back and went to answer. "Baker. . . . Yes, sir. Right away." He set down the telephone and turned to me.

"Rutherford wants me. I've got to go. But I'll be back later. You'd better have a convincing story for me when I come back. And if he has found out about Mrs. Rutherford's disappearance, you had better hope I never come back." Rage boiled up in him and he struck me, unleashing all his fury.

Then he took out a big pocket knife. When he saw my appalled expression he laughed. He bent over and cut the telephone wire, went out of the room, and came back with towels, with which he tied my feet together, then my wrists. Finally he bent and kissed me, a long deliberate kiss from which I shrank. Then he gagged me.

He removed the billfold from my handbag, said mockingly, "See you soon, sweetheart," and went out, closing and locking the door behind him. There was a click as the padlock was fastened.

I heard him run lightly down the uncarpeted stairs and slam the door.

"What I need is a Houdini," I thought. My hands had been tied together but at least they were tied in front of me rather than behind my back. He had been in a hurry, of course, and he had been near panic, too, because of Rutherford's unexpected call and Mrs. Rutherford's escape. He had probably been wondering whether Rutherford was going to accuse him of having some part in that escape. I think he would almost have preferred that to the knowledge that he had been duped, he, the great Max.

I looked longingly at the telephone, but the wire had been cut. First things first, I decided, and stood up. As soon as I started to move, I lost my balance and toppled back on the chair. I tried again. It was extraordinary to discover how hard it was to balance. Then, very carefully, I began to move in slow hops. One loss of balance sent me staggering against a chair, which I overturned, but I made it to the kitchen door, edging slowly along the wall for support. I pushed it open. The kitchen was dimly lighted from a court. I found the light switch and turned it on. The kitchen had every conceivable appliance. Max was getting a lot of money from somewhere, money that he enjoyed spending. I believed some sense of the dramatic had made him choose as unlikely a place as this rundown apartment building to transform into his personal idea of grandeur. Or, of course, he wanted to escape suspicion by keeping his luxurious way of life a secret from his employer.

Hop. Hop. Hop. This was risky work on the waxed tiles of the kitchen floor. One skid here and I'd have an awful time getting up. I made it to the side with the counters and, using them for a support, moved along until I came to the drawers. The first held table silver, the second a variety of kitchen cooking forks, spatulas, egg beaters, and so forth. The third held knives. I pulled out a sharp carving knife, which dropped out of my bound hands. I bent over, lost my balance, and toppled on the floor, the knife under me.

I rolled on my side until I could reach it and finally managed to sit up, my back to the cabinet, knees drawn up, and clamped the knife between my knees, gripping hard. Then I began to saw at the towel that tied my wrists. The knife slipped and I started again. How often that happened I don't know. Toward the end I discovered in shame that I was crying, the tears dripping down my cheeks. And then, when I had almost given up hope, the last threads severed and my hands were free. They were also dead white; the circulation had stopped.

There was no use trying to pick up the knife until I could restore some feeling. At length, after beating my hands on my thighs, I felt a painful tingling and the color began to seep back. I rubbed my hands together, flexed my fingers, and, though they still hurt, I could use them.

First I pulled off the beastly gag and then untied the towel that bound my feet, as this was easier than sawing through the heavy material — at least a bit easier, for my fingers were still awkward.

When I had finally made it to my feet I stood quite still for a few moments until my dizziness was gone. A look around the kitchen revealed no escape route from there. A single window looked out on a dimly lighted court, across which I could see lighted windows. People watched television or talked or read with their windows closed against the winter night. Even if I had called they could not have heard me above the incessant beat of rock and roll from the third floor, that monotonous blast of sound that satisfies the ears of the uncivilized, at least when they are partially numbed by dope.

The bedroom was another example of

Max's fantasy world. He must, I thought, be a devotee of the late, late movies. The bed-spread was shocking pink satin and there were shocking pink draperies at the windows. The rugs were black velvet, and beside the bed there was a white bearskin rug. And, as I had expected, there was the Queen Carlotta dressing table, ridiculous in a man's room.

# 12

I began to get some very odd ideas about Max. Because of his air of assured masculinity and his potent sex appeal, I had taken the façade for the real man. No doubt he victimized women only as a part of his stock in trade. I doubted if women played much part in his real life.

And then, as a challenge to my theory, I was aware of the faint scent of Channel Number Five. It was stronger beside the dressing table, and I pulled open a drawer in which I found a small assortment of cosmetics and a perfume bottle in which only a few drops remained, a bottle from which the stopper was missing. I had noticed that scent earlier in the day. But where? And then I recalled being aware of it from the open door of Rose Miller's room.

Now I set myself to search in earnest. If Rose had been in Max's rooms, it was possible that Mary Ann had been there, too. There was nothing of hers in any drawer; nothing in the clothes closet, which held an extensive and expensive wardrobe belonging to Max. If he had any proofs of his relationship with Mary Ann, he would keep it.

Only when I lifted the dressing table bench and turned it over, did I find the snapshot, fastened on with cellophane tape. And there was a naked Mary Ann, stepping out of a bathtub, half startled, half smiling. My impulse was to take the photo with me, but only in its actual position was it the proof I needed. I left it where it was.

I opened the satin curtains at the windows with a tug on the cord and my heart leaped. The one thing I had hoped for was true. I had remembered from the time before Jimmy and I rented the apartment above the shop that we, too, had lived in a reconstructed tenement, with an ugly fire escape across the back wall. And there it was.

I pulled up one of the windows and stepped out cautiously onto the fire escape, a shaky affair that probably had not been checked for safety since the building had been erected. In the dim light from the court I could see the section that rose to the third floor landing and then to the roof. I made my way cautiously to the open end, trying to recall how these things work. The section that dropped to the ground was pulled up to the second-floor level to prevent intruders from getting into the building. One's weight dropped it to the ground.

I took one step in the dark, missed, and my leg flailed in the air. The lower section of the fire escape had rusted. It refused to budge.

I stood there for a long time, not knowing what to do. I peered down in the darkness, but I could not see how far the drop was. I remembered that the stairs I had climbed with Max had not been steep, fifteen feet at most. But fifteen feet in the dark! And to let myself down, falling into space . . . But there wasn't, after all, any choice. To go back would be to fall into Max's hands. On the whole I preferred to take a chance. I drew a long breath and dropped.

I struck the hard pavement with a terrific jar and felt a shock of pain from my right heel up to my hip, up to my neck, up to the top of my head. My whole right side hurt as though it had been burned. My right wrist — my hand had been extended to break my fall — seemed to be broken.

One thing was sure. I had to get up, die of exposure, or be caught by Max. There weren't many choices and all of them were impossible.

With the help of my left hand, I managed to push myself up and stumbled against the side of the building, almost blacking out when my right foot touched the pavement. I couldn't move. No one could expect me to move. I wanted to lie down on the pavement and howl. But in times of stress, as men discover in war, you can do the impossible. Groping along the wall, hopping on my left foot, though every move jolted me and sent pain rushing through my body, I worked my way toward a door that had a dim light over it. I had to stand there a long time, after being ignominiously sick, before I could turn the knob with my left hand. Still at that slow crawl, I made my way along the dim passage to the front of the building.

## II

I had nearly reached it when a door opened and a boy about twelve, with bright red hair and freckles, wearing jeans and a turtleneck sweater, looked out. For a moment he stood gaping at me, and then he said, "You're hurt. You'd better come in." He took my right arm and I yelped.

"Gee, I'm sorry." He was anxious, but he was excited, too. He led me into a shabby living room dominated by a television screen showing a gangster film. He switched it off and said, "My mother has gone to spend the evening with her sister. I don't know . . . Should I get you a doctor or something?"

"How did you know I was outside?"

"I heard this scream and a thud, but there was so much noise on the screen I wasn't sure. And then there is always so much noise from the top floor we get so we don't pay much attention. But I got to thinking I had better see if anything was wrong. Gee, you look really awful!"

There was a mirror over the television set, arranged to make the cramped little room look larger, and I stared in disbelief at my battered face. It was swollen and discolored. But that wasn't the worst, of course. The worst was the agony that shot through my right side, from my ankle to my head.

"Have you a telephone?"

"Sure. Shall I call our doctor?"

There was no time for a doctor. Only one thing mattered, Mrs. Rutherford's safety. With Rutherford demanding Max, who had the key to her place of safety, not one more minute could be lost, if it was not already too late. I had wasted a lot of time getting free, searching the bedroom, and building up courage to jump.

I smiled at the eager face. "Not yet. Can you dial a number for me?"

He sat on the floor beside me, the telephone on his lap. He hadn't asked a single question except to know whether he could help. If I had a son I would like him to be just like this one. I gave him Philip's number.

The phone was answered so quickly I thought Philip must have been sitting beside it.

"Philip, this is Jennifer. Did she get there all right?"

"Yes, she's here, but where are you? I tried the shop and the apartment, but Jenks said he hadn't heard from you. No names mentioned, of course. I understood from Mrs. Rutherford that you were going to 'some shop.' That's all she seemed to know. Where in hell are you?"

"First, I've got to tell you something, Philip."

"But —"

"Listen to me! She isn't safe there."

"Of course, she is safe here."

"Please listen," I said desperately. I was fighting down a blackness that threatened to overcome me. "The chauffeur, Max, stole my letter to you. He knows your address. I should have thought of that before I sent her there. You've got to get her away."

"But —"

"Philip!"

At the desperation in my voice he said quietly, "Okay, darling. Go ahead."

"Max has been called up to Rutherford's now. They'll know — at least Max knows already — that she got away. If Rutherford comes for her, you can't possibly keep her there. After all, she is his wife. And it might make things worse for Jimmy. Rutherford is capable of anything. He might even have you arrested for kidnapping her. I tell you —"

"All right. Keep your shirt on. I'll get her out in an hour."

"Where?"

"I'll think of something. Where are you, Jennifer? I warn you I'm not making a move until I know where and how you are. You sound darned queer to me."

His devotion had never seemed so ill-timed. It was action I wanted, not personal concern.

"I'm all right. I'll call you later."

The boy took the telephone away from me and put it back in its cradle. "Gosh!" he said in a low tone. "Gosh! Kidnapping and everything! And you look awful, miss. Can't I do anything?"

I couldn't go to Philip's. I couldn't go to the shop. Then I thought of Hilda's prize-fighter. That was the man I needed right now. But I couldn't go to her house because I didn't have a penny. Max had taken care of that.

"Will you do something for me?" I asked.

"Of course," the boy said promptly, still watching me anxiously.

"Will you call this number?"

He did so and again held the telephone for me. "May I speak to Hilda?" I asked the man who answered the telephone.

"Who wants her?" he asked suspiciously.

"Tell her it's Mary Ann Weldone. She said I could call her if I was in trouble, and I am — awful trouble."

In a moment I heard Hilda's voice. "Miss Weldone, what is wrong?"

"Max trailed me tonight and brought me to his apartment by force. It was awful. And then Rutherford called him and he went away, taking my billfold, leaving me bound and gagged, and cutting the telephone wire. I got free and fell off the fire escape, and a nice boy let me telephone from his apartment. Could someone come for me? I haven't any money, and anyhow I don't really think I can walk without help."

After a brief colloquy with Hilda, the man was on the telephone again. "What's that address, Miss Weldone?" He sounded brisk and businesslike and competent.

I asked the boy and relayed the number.

"Which apartment?"

"The first on the left on the ground floor."

"I'll be there in fifteen minutes. Keep the door locked, and don't let anyone in until I come."

"Thank you." Once the boy had put the telephone down, I sagged against the couch, with a feeling that the marines had landed and everything was under control. Hilda's fiancé exuded confidence.

The boy's eyes seemed as big as footballs and blazed with excitement. He got up to lock the door and then came to stand beside me in a protective attitude. I tried to smile at him.

## III

The pain in my right side when I was lifted off the floor brought me around, moaning. I was in the arms of the largest young man I had ever seen, tall and broad and strong. I'm not so awfully light, but I felt like a feather in his arms. He had blunt features that weren't handsome but nice. Beside him stood the red-haired boy, who was no longer interested in me. He was staring at the big young man with a look of absolute worship.

"You're Big Jack Logan," he breathed.

Jack grinned at him. "That's right."

"Gosh! Oh, gosh! What a night! The kids will never believe it. Could I have your autograph?"

Jack said, "Well, I'll have to wait until I put the young lady down."

He laughed at that. "Oh, sure. Of course. I only thought . . ."

I thought I was speaking loudly, but the words came out in a sort of whisper. "I hope you don't mind me calling, but I thought — a prizefighter. . . ."

The pleasant face wasn't so pleasant, after all. He set me gently in a chair and wiped the perspiration off my face with a big clean handkerchief. "What did the . . ." He swallowed. "What did he do to you? Your face!"

"He struck me. But that wasn't the worst. I fell off the fire escape, and I think my ankle is broken. I feel as though all of me is broken."

"I'll take you home," Jack decided. "We have a lot of room. My sister May is planning to turn the old place into a rooming house when Hilda and I get married. I have a doctor who makes house calls, and he'll fix you up. Hilda thinks you are swell. So do I. We owe you a lot for that bonus check."

"But that was Mrs. Rutherford."

"Miss Miller had already told Hilda she was fired and that she would get two-weeks' salary. But now we can get married right away. After I've taken care of you. I'm going to look for that guy."

"Not yet," I said. "Not yet. First we've got to make sure Mrs. Rutherford is all right."

Jack considered the matter deliberately. Physically he was lightning swift, but his mental processes were ponderous and not to be hurried. "Okay," he agreed. He turned to my red-haired friend. "What's your name, kid?"

"Tom O'Connor."

"I want you to give me a helping hand, Tom."

"Sure thing."

"Hold open this door and the outside door, and then unlock the passenger's door on that little VW out there. Can you do that?"

"You bet, Mr. Logan."

"Jack," Jack told him, and the boy's face was like a rising sun.

He swallowed. "Sure, Jack."

"And write down your name and address for me. I want you to have a couple of ring-side seats for my next fight. Think you can make it?"

Tom's face was all grin, like a Hallowe'en pumpkin.

Much to my relief I fell into blessed darkness before I was settled in the car, and the pain faded into nothing. It was pain again that roused me when something gripped my right ankle.

"Okay," said a brisk voice. "It isn't broken." I looked up into the lean, tired face of a young man who wore horn-rimmed glasses and had a stethoscope around his neck. "Just a sprain. But you've sure taken a beating. You'd better let Logan teach you self-defense." The grin faded. "That was a bad beating, wasn't it?"

I nodded, and even that hurt because my neck was stiff. "What's wrong?"

"You've got a couple of cracked ribs, a sprained ankle, a sprained wrist, and multiple bruises, but you're going to live. Just try to stay out of scraps." He was smiling, but his eyes were serious.

He stood up. "Okay, Hilda. She's all yours now. You know what you have to do: the pain killer in an hour, and then one every three hours, but only when they are really necessary. If she develops a fever or anything like that, give me a ring."

He went out of the room, and I heard a brief altercation in another room. The prizefighter was arguing with his doctor friend. The latter said firmly, "Keep out of this. You've done your bit. Let the girl decide for herself how she wants it handled, whether the police or —"

"I don't need the police to handle my affairs," Jack raged.

"No, you need Hilda to handle them. Just remember: never get in a fight you aren't being paid for."

I tried desperately to say something and realized that Hilda was trying to quiet me.

"Hilda, please call this number." I gave her Philip's number. "Say I'm all right."

She raised her brows and smiled in amusement. "All right?"

"Well, safe anyhow. Safe with you."

"That's for sure. No one can get near you. Jack is breathing fire. But don't worry about that. I'll make him see reason."

# 13

And then it was thirty-six hours later. The interim was almost a complete blank, with moments of pain when the doctor prodded my ankle, bandaged my wrist, and checked on my multiple bruises.

I woke up all at once, clear-headed, to find Hilda standing beside the bed, taking my pulse.

"Hello," I said.

"Well, welcome back!" She smiled down at me and there was a kind of amused sympathy in her smile. I groped with my left hand when she had released it and felt my face, which was stiff and swollen. I found it difficult to focus on Hilda.

"What's wrong with my eyes?" I asked in a panic.

"Brace yourself." She brought me a mirror, and I stared in horror at the swollen, discolored face and the puffy blackened eyes. "Oh, no!"

She laughed. "I know how you feel."

"You haven't the faintest idea how I feel."

"How about some breakfast?"

I accepted so enthusiastically that she went out of the room laughing. When she returned she was accompanied by Jack's sister, Mary, carrying a tray on which I saw, to my delight, bacon and eggs and toast and coffee. My mouth was painful but it didn't prevent me from eating, and I never stopped until I had cleared off everything. The two girls watched in amusement, but with pleasure, too.

When the older one had removed the tray and Hilda was trying, with gentle hands, to wash my face and brush my hair without hurting me too much, I said, "You've both been incredibly kind, and there was no reason for doing it. I had no right to call on you."

"Considering that you are indirectly responsible for the fact that Jack and I can be married six months sooner than we hoped — and he was tickled to have you call on him for help — so anyhow — I guess we are even."

Cautiously she helped me raise myself a trifle on pillows. I bit back a moan.

"Sorry. That hurt, didn't it? But I thought you'd be more comfortable in a different position."

I nodded, unable to speak until the waves of pain subsided.

At last Hilda, who had been watching me, nodded, aware that the worst of it was over. "I guess now you are ready for some news."

I turned my head quickly and winced. There didn't seem to be any part of me that didn't hurt. "Bad news?" I pulled myself up higher on the pillows. "Mrs. Rutherford?"

"Now, now. First there was a call from a guy who said he was Jimmy. That's all. Just Jimmy. He wanted to know what you were doing here. Well, Jack didn't know much, of course, except that Max had roughed you up and you'd fallen off a fire escape, but he told him the best he could and said the doctor had assured him there was nothing seriously wrong."

I moaned in protest, and Hilda laughed at me.

"He wanted you to call back the first thing in the morning but, of course, you weren't awake then. So when he called again, I told him you were still unconscious. He swore and said he couldn't leave there, wherever it was, and another guy, Philip Banning or Hanning or something like that couldn't come either. He was being followed wherever he went, and he didn't want to lead anyone to you.

"And then," Hilda hesitated, and I had the curious feeling that she was editing what she was about to say, "and then I got a real scare when Mr. Rutherford's assistant, or whatever he is, showed up. You know, that Mr. Preston."

206

Her eyes were bright with curiosity. "He was in a state. I never saw him before when he wasn't as cool as could be. He said he had found out where you were from your Uncle Bert. He just put me to one side and barged in here to see you for himself."

"With me looking like this?" I wailed.

Hilda's eyes widened.

"What did he want?" I asked.

"He wanted to see with his own eyes that you were all right. When he got a good look at you — God! The man looked murderous. Max had better keep out of his way. I wouldn't have thought him a match for Max, but — I don't know."

"Did he say anything about Mrs. Rutherford? Is she all right?"

"He just looked at you for a long time, and then he bent over and kissed your forehead and told me to take care of you and keep you safe and asked if I needed any money — and then he went away."

"And he didn't tell you about Max or Mrs. Rutherford or anything?"

"He said Rutherford had discovered that his wife was missing, and he called Max and had him drive him out that night."

"Well?" I knew I sounded feverish, but I couldn't bear the suspense.

Hilda couldn't evade any more. "Max

drove him," she said miserably, "to Mr. Hanning's house." She added, almost in reproach, "I didn't know Mr. Preston was told about Mrs. Rutherford's escape."

So the time had come to drop the role of Mary Ann Weldone and I told her the whole story. Now and then, particularly, when I revealed that Mary Ann's husband was my brother and when I spoke of her pregnancy and Max's assumed part in it — and the source of the sleeping pills that had ended her problems — Hilda gasped. But she never interrupted. Then I told her about the campaign to destroy my brother, Jimmy, and how Philip Hanning had helped me adopt the personality of Mary Ann Weldone and how Forrest Preston had stumbled onto the truth when he found me lunching with Uncle Bert.

"Well," she said at last. "Well." She groped for other words and found them inadequate. "Well!"

II

All morning I lay in bed wondering what had happened to Mrs. Rutherford, whether Philip had been obliged to surrender her to her husband, whether she had met Jimmy, and, if so, how she had liked him and what any of us could do now.

I was so incapacitated for the time being that I could not get around without help. About one o'clock, when I had finished a bowl of homemade soup that would have put heart into a man awaiting execution, and an omelet as light as a cloud, with two butter-drenched muffins — there was nothing wrong with my appetite — someone rang the doorbell. Jack was working out with a sparring partner somewhere, and there was no one in the old house on the edge of the Bronx but the two women and myself. Hilda, who had picked up my tray, stood motionless, listening. Jack's sister, May, who had been teasing me about my appetite, startled me by opening a dresser drawer and taking out a small revolver. I stared at her, mouth agape.

"This house has been broken into three times, twice by burglars and once by a couple of young vandals. Jack got me this revolver and I was taught how to use it on the police firing range, so it is all right. I have a permit, and I'd never shoot except in self-defense."

As the bell rang again, more insistently, she went to open it on a chain, her right hand in her pocket on the revolver.

Then she said, "Oh, it's you again! I guess you can come in."

"How is she?"

At the sound of that voice, I sat bolt upright, groaning and saying in a furious mutter, "I can't see him, not looking like this," but it was too late. May came in, followed by Forrest Preston, as calm as usual, giving the impression of looking down his nose at the world. His hair was smooth as glass.

He came to stand beside the bed and he didn't after all, look like a camel. At least I never heard of a camel with eyes like that, so intent, so anxious.

"Hello," I said and moved my left hand, which he clasped in his own.

Hilda and May exchanged glances and went out, drawing the door almost closed behind them. Forrest stood holding my hand, looking at my disfigured face. He didn't move or say anything.

"Won't you sit down?" I said at last. And then he released my hand and pulled a chair close to the bed. "Is it all right for you to be here? I mean, does Rutherford know?"

"Thanks to Lord Glydes running interference, my respected employer is lunching with him at the Plaza today. Night before last I thought he was going berserk when he found out, through Mrs. Rutherford's secretary, that his wife had disappeared. He sent for Max, who said he had been double-crossed by you and that he had driven Mrs. Rutherford to the

Waldorf, thinking, of course, she was you, as she wore your coat and dark glasses and she was carrying one of your suitcases, with Hilda carrying the other."

"Poor Hilda!"

"Well, all this was being put in the most careful words for my benefit. The poor woman must have cracked mentally. She was being victimized by you. She must be found for her own safety. And so forth. And so forth. Far into the night.

"Well, I figured, knowing you and your obsession about the woman's safety, that you must have the situation well in hand. I knew, of course, that she lacked the initiative to do anything on her own. Then Max said he had mailed a letter for you — I rather liked that touch — and he just happened to remember the address. At least it was some place to start looking. And then Rutherford remembered that Hanning was the name of one of your references. By the way, did you ever find out who is doing Max's spying for him at the apartment?"

"Yes, Rose Miller."

"Miller!" Forrest laughed. "Well, I'll be damned. The woman must be forty-five."

"That's cruel of you," I said. "I was cruel, too."

"Cruel!"

"A middle-aged woman can fall in love."

"She is about as alluring as a head of cabbage."

"What's that got to do with it? Do you think only pretty women are interested in men?"

Forrest laughed again. "Does it occur to you that you are defending a woman who would have sold you down the river?"

I made no reply and after a quick, questioning glance, as though trying to assess my mood, Forrest took up his story.

"Well, Max drove Rutherford up to Hanning's house, and I got on the telephone to warn him that he was about to be invaded. He said you had already called him, and then I heard him say, 'What's that?' He came back and said, 'The enemy has been sighted.' "

"Hurry. Go on."

The rest of the story consisted of telephone calls made at judicious intervals to Philip's house by Forrest. The situation was a stand-off. Rutherford had gone to the door and demanded his wife. Philip had refused to admit him. When Rutherford threatened him with the police, Philip politely invited him to go right ahead, which, of course, was the last thing Rutherford wanted. Then Rutherford claimed that his wife was out of her mind and he'd bring up Dr. Reynolds to take care of her. Philip said he was sure Mrs. Rutherford would agree, provided she could have a psychiatrist of her own choice examine her before Reynolds was permitted to take her away.

By this time Rutherford was ripe for murder. After a lot of talk and a lot of threats, he drove off in a taxi and Max settled down to wait in the Lincoln. About an hour later, two men showed up in a Chevrolet, parked behind the Lincoln, and came up to talk to Max. Then they took over the watch and Max drove off.

"And then," I interrupted for the first time, "Max went back to his apartment and found that I had escaped."

Forrest drew a long rasping breath before he could go on talking. Then he said, his voice as calm as ever, that Rutherford's men were still watching Philip's house in relays, so it was impossible to get Mrs. Rutherford away. On the other hand, they could not get in without violence, which Rutherford didn't want. Philip had gone about his regular business, reporting to his office as usual, with one of Rutherford's henchmen on his trail, which was why he hadn't dared come to see me.

"Poor Philip! What an awful amount of

trouble I've got him into, if nothing worse."

"I think he is enjoying it. Damn it," Forrest exploded, "I'd give an arm to be a part of the action instead of sitting on the sidelines like this. It is maddening! No, your friend Hanning is having himself a whale of a time."

Forrest glanced toward the window. "You may not have noticed, but we've had a heavy rain, mixed with sleet, for the past twenty-four hours. Hanning reports that at his regular lunch time he took a brisk walk — he has a heavy, lined waterproof coat, and his tail didn't even have a raincoat. He's in hopes the guy has caught pneumonia."

I laughed; then I sobered. "But Max won't enjoy being beaten by a woman. He won't like that at all." I wanted to cry out that I was afraid of Max, but I was ashamed to do it. And, after all, whatever happened to me, I had asked for it.

"Tell me about Max," Forrest said. "What I learned from Hanning and Jack Logan — is that Big Jack, the prizefighter? — and from Mrs. Rutherford's former maid was awfully jumbled."

I described Mrs. Rutherford's escape and how Max had left her at the Waldorf, thinking that he was delivering me. We had planned that she was to go through the basement passage to the underground taxi stand and drive to Philip's house. Obviously she had managed that successfully.

Then Hilda had steered me out of the apartment through the kitchen, given me her phone number in case of need, and I had taken a Fifth Avenue bus, intending to go to the shop and leave Jenks free to return to Philip's house.

I described how Max had forced me into the Lincoln and afterwards into his apartment. I broke off to give him a highly colored picture of that unlikely apartment and to say that, if any proof had been needed of Max's participation in Jimmy's problems, the presence of the Sisley and the Queen Carlotta dressing table were sufficient evidence. Then I described finding the snapshot of a naked Mary Ann.

Something in Forrest's expression, though he did not say a word while I was talking, warned me to treat as lightly as I could the way Max had struck me and left me bound and gagged when Rutherford sent for him. I didn't mention the kiss at all. For the first time I understood Hilda's comment about the man being potentially dangerous. Something in his very controlled quietness was like a lighted time fuse.

"And then I jumped off the fire escape," I

said, "and fell a long way and landed on concrete and got sort of battered, and that nice boy rescued me and telephoned for Big Jack and — that's all."

## III

"Quite a saga," Forrest said, but his voice was shaking. He picked up my left hand, looked at it front and back, and then kissed it tightly. I knew then what I should have known from the beginning, what Uncle Bert had sensed. But if my first reaction was a kind of incredulous delight, my second was one of remorse about Philip.

I tugged at my hand and Forrest released it immediately. One thing, I told myself, he must really love me if he could bear to look at my swollen, discolored face and two black eyes reduced to slits.

"What happens next?" I asked.

"Right now it's a stalemate. Rutherford can't get his wife out of Hanning's house without a first-rate scandal, which would ruin his prospects. Obviously she can't stay there indefinitely. Max must be going out of his mind, wondering what has happened to you and where you fit into all this. He won't have understood your references to Uncle

Bert and the camel" — he caught my side-long glance and we both laughed — "but he does know you tricked him when you arranged for Mrs. Rutherford's getaway with him driving the car. That's a touch he won't appreciate."

"It was my fault. When he hurt me like that I yelled and told him the truth. I was ashamed, but I just didn't have the guts."

"What did he do?" Forrest's voice was hoarse.

So I told him, as I had sworn myself that I would not. I saw him struggling with his temper. At last he said, "One thing that baffles me is why Rutherford is so terrified of having his wife off the leash."

"That must be because of the tape."

"Tell me that part again. I didn't get the story clearly the first time; I was so preoccupied with your high-handed plan for getting Mrs. Rutherford away."

So I did, explaining about the tape Mary Ann had stumbled on which Rutherford apparently had put with some other tapes on the theory that one daisy is lost in a field of daisies.

"But why keep the daisy if it's so dangerous?"

"Because it involves someone else, someone high up. Mrs. Rutherford was afraid to tell me who he was. Perhaps Rutherford is holding that tape over the head of the other man."

Obviously Mary Ann had not understood what the thing meant and had mentioned it to her father as a joke. That was when he had put her in Dr. Reynolds' sanitarium, hoping that after the good doctor had worked on her and time had elapsed she would have forgotten the whole thing. And her incarceration was a reminder to her mother that it would be unsafe for her to reveal her own knowledge. But Mrs. Rutherford remained a potential danger because, even after more than twenty years of marriage, she still knew so little about her husband that she had attempted to remonstrate with him about his unethical dealings.

"To put it in a nice way," Forrest said grimly, "any rumor that he is unloading his fortune in Swiss banks would raise merry hell for him. Any other little tidbits?"

"Well, Max must be the blackmailer. You should see his apartment. It must have cost an awful lot to decorate, and he has a wardrobe filled with expensive clothes. And now that we have proof Mary Ann was there, I feel sure he's the baby's father, and she undoubtedly told him the whole story about the funny mix-up with the tapes. She might not have understood their implication, but she knew they sent her to the sanitarium."

"Well, well!" Forrest bent over and kissed me lightly on both cheeks. "That's your Girl Scout medal. Now if there is any such thing as fool's luck, I'll find that tape."

"What is your real concern in all this, Forrest?"

He realized that I had to know. "Government. There is a lot going on that doesn't get in the papers, Jennifer. The investigations into corruption didn't end with Watergate. You might even say they just began there. And now, after everyone trying to keep you in the clear, you've provided the best lead I've had up to now." He glanced at his watch. "I've got to get back to the apartment. Are you safe here?"

"Jack's sister has a gun, and she knows how to use it. And Jack comes home at night. He's as good as an army."

"Has it occurred to you that Max might come here? If he saw you with Hilda, he'll figure out she was involved in Mrs. Rutherford's escape and he can easily discover where she lives. Miss Miller must have addresses for all the staff."

I laughed. "I have a feeling that Jack is praying that Max will come here, not just because of what he did to me, but because he's been making unwelcome passes at Hilda. He can't endure thinking that any woman can resist him."

Forrest grinned. "If Big Jack Logan is as good as they say he is, I could almost feel sorry for Max." He looked at my swollen eyes again. "Almost. Well, I'll keep in touch."

"Will you — tell Philip?" I asked hesitantly.

"Tell him?"

"That I'm all right." But that wasn't what I had meant to say.

"I'll tell him that I have seen you. Of course he can't risk your safety by coming here. He is naturally worried."

"Poor Philip!"

Forrest looked down at me with a curiously intent expression, hesitated, and then went out of the room with a little salute. I heard his voice as he spoke to the two girls, and then he was gone.

# 14

That afternoon Hilda called Philip's house and got Jimmy, who hammered questions at her and seemed to be enraged because, although he was well enough to go back to the shop, he was unable to get out of the house on account of the twenty-four hour watch being kept by Rutherford's hatchet men. Anyhow, some man had to stay on the spot to protect Mrs. Rutherford.

Hilda was kept busy running back and forth from the telephone to my bed carrying messages and questions. Finally, in spite of her protests, I persuaded her to help me get out of bed and propel me to the telephone. My right ankle hurt like the devil and my right side was painful when I moved. I subsided on the couch beside the telephone table, sweating and sick, but I had made it.

"We've got ourselves into a damned mess," Jimmy said gloomily. "I'm stuck here. You're stuck there. I take it you have an adequate guard in that prizefighter."

"The best. You needn't worry about me."

"Oh, it's not me," Jimmy said cheerfully.

"I know you always land on your feet — always have. But Philip is worried sick. When this is over you had better marry the guy, Jen. You couldn't do better. He has practically turned his house into a port of missing men for you, and now it is under siege and the poor devil is followed everywhere he goes. It's a good thing he stands so high with that outfit he is in, or he'd probably be out on his ear now as a suspicious character. Anyhow you can't go on playing fast and loose with him much longer."

"I'm not playing fast and loose with him," I said indignantly. "I've never even encouraged him. You know that. Heaven knows I am grateful, but that is all there is to it."

There was silence at the other end of the phone. Then Jimmy said tentatively, "I'm not very observant about people, Jen, but it occurs to me . . . well, there was something about that man Preston when he called, a sort of implied priority where you are concerned. Is that the spanner in the works?"

"But when he called you I didn't even know —" I broke off. "I'm sorry about Philip, Jimmy."

"Yes," he said heavily. "So am I. Sorry and considerably ashamed of accepting his hospitality and help under false pretenses."

"Jimmy!"

"One thing sure, you've got to break the bad news yourself. I won't have any part in it. I hope you know what you are doing. Sometimes people go off half-cocked, get swept off their feet. I know because it happened to me. And you could be mistaken, too." His voice grew fainter as he turned away from the telephone. "Yes, it's my sister. Jen, Mrs. Rutherford wants to speak to you."

At first I hardly recognized her, because her voice had a ring, a kind of vibrancy. "My dear, why didn't you tell me about your brother and Mary Ann? If I had only known! I like him so much, and he would have been so good for her and I could have helped them both."

She couldn't, of course, because nothing would have made Mary Ann a fit companion for Jimmy or have taught her to face life. But Mrs. Rutherford had regained her confidence — or had attained a brand-new confidence, which was the important thing.

"And your delightful friend, Mr. Hanning, has made me feel so welcome, even with those awful men waiting outside to prevent me from getting away. I feel so safe with Mr. Hanning, Mary Ann — no, I mean Jennifer. It's a wonderful feeling to be safe. Safe and protected."

"What are your plans?"

"I don't know," she said blithely. "I'm leaving it to Mr. Hanning and to Jimmy. And when this is all over and I am free of Paul — yes, I'm going to divorce him — and when you are married to Mr. Hanning, I'm going to see lots and lots of you and of Jimmy, who is practically my own son."

Poor Jimmy, I thought, and then I realized that the hold of other people on him was always tenuous, like grasping smoke. He would be gentle with her, but he simply would not be there in any real sense. People like Jimmy miss a lot of the big emotions of living, but they escape a lot of emotional problems, too.

I set down the telephone and leaned back on the couch, unwilling to start the return trip to bed until I had rested. Jimmy had taken for granted that I would marry Philip. So had Mrs. Rutherford. And, after all, Forrest had not asked me to marry him. He had not even said he loved me. He had kissed me as impersonally as though I were a six-month-old baby.

I was startled when the telephone rang beside me. May came to answer it and said, "Who? Miss Bartlett? I'm afraid there is no one . . . Lord Glydes?" She arched her brows in question. I nodded my head emphatically and held out my left hand for the phone.

"Uncle Bert?"

"This is becoming more Holmesian every minute," he assured me. "Escapes. Disguises. Kidnapping. I take it you were kidnapped. The whole thing is such bad melodrama that I refuse to believe in it."

"That must be nice for you," I said dryly.

"Sorry, my dear, I'm not really taking this preposterous situation as lightly as you may think."

"I know. How did you enjoy your luncheon?"

"My — oh, I gather Preston has been in touch with you. Yes, well, the man Rutherford is quite definitely a wrong one. I'd say he is the kind who would automatically choose the crooked way even if the straight one were more profitable. Bland with a grain of coarseness showing through. Arrogant with inferiority seething under it. He even assured me that I would profit by sponsoring his social career in England. It took all that Britain phlegm we are said to have to keep me from kicking his bottom."

"I hope," I said as solemnly as I could, "that the whole experience proves valuable to you."

He snorted. Then he laughed. "At least I have enough on him to spike his guns. He'll never get that appointment as ambassador. This I am going to enjoy."

"I never knew you to be vindictive."

"I never before had a niece beaten up and kidnapped, or a nephew whose business is being ruined and whose reputation is being smeared, or known of a woman hiding from her husband to prevent her from being locked up in a private asylum. Men like Rutherford have to be stopped, my dear."

"And you think he will be?"

"Of course." Uncle Bert sounded shocked. "Of course he will. When the evidence is all in he won't be left with a leg to stand on."

"The evidence exists if we can just find it." I gave him a hasty rundown of the missing tape, and he muttered to himself.

"What happens next?" I asked him. "What do we do now?"

"You," he said firmly, "have done your job. You sit back and recuperate." When I was silent he repeated, "Is that clear, Jennifer?"

"Yes," I said slowly.

"Promise?"

"How can I? I don't know what may happen, what I might have to do."

He sighed. But Uncle Bert was not one to beat a dead horse. "At least, be careful, my dear. Be very careful."

# II

Three days later the situation was unchanged. I was recuperating at the house of Jack's sister, May, walking with the help of a stick, and the black around my eyes was fading. But the situation was still a standoff. Jimmy and Mrs. Rutherford were unable to leave Philip's house; and Forrest, kept hopping by Rutherford's demands and his own private activities, did not return to see me, though he telephoned several times a day, as did Philip. The latter always assured me cheerfully that his guests were well and happy and he enjoyed having them. If there was a growing reserve in his manner, it was unstressed. Philip had always been sensitive to my moods, and I thought he was becoming aware of my attitude. I almost hoped he would, because I was coward enough to shrink from having to tell him that I could not marry him, though I knew, of course, that he would make no demands while I was under such a burden of gratitude. No woman, it seemed to me in moments of depression, had even made such unscrupulous use of a man as I had of Philip, aware as I had been from the beginning that what he had done had been for love of me.

Jimmy had not called me again, so I

grasped that he had not forgiven me because of what must have seemed to be my ingratitude and treachery. I was ashamed. I argued myself blue in the face, assuring myself that it would only be a disservice to marry Philip when I did not love him. But I understood, too, understood clearly, why Jimmy was resentful of me for hurting Philip. I hated it, but there was nothing I could do about it. My very bones seemed to melt when I thought of Forrest. I didn't know him well. I had talked with him only a few times. I had started by disliking him actively. So there was no accounting for my present state.

"You're a besotted little idiot," I told myself savagely. But I didn't listen to myself.

That morning Big Jack enlivened us by talking about his fight the night before and the red-haired boy watching goggle-eyed and bringing a friend to meet the great fighter. It was easy to see how glamorous the good-natured giant had made that evening for a child, a night he would never forget. It occurred to me that Hilda was a lucky girl. The future stretched ahead bright and clear for her.

Sometime later Jack set off for some scheduled interviews with the press under the auspices of his manager. Hilda left to get a permanent wave, so she would have time for one shampoo and set before her marriage. It was with some reluctance that May left me alone while she did some marketing.

"Having a man like Jack to feed," she pretended to grumble, "takes as much food as it does to run a small restaurant. Sure you'll be all right?"

I laughed. "Of course I'm sure."

"If I didn't have to do it this morning — especially when Hilda is away — I wouldn't dream of leaving you alone, but I have a contractor coming this afternoon to discuss the changes we'll have to make when I turn this barracks into a paying rooming house, and I can't afford to miss him. One thing I've sworn to myself is that I'll never be dependent on Jack when he marries. He will kick like a steer and so will Hilda, bless her heart, but I'm determined to look after myself and pay my own way."

"You run along and don't worry about me."

May was still vacillating. "I'll tell you what. I'll give you my gun."

"I'd be a lot more afraid of that than of anyone trying to get in. Anyhow, who would try?"

"You'll be sure to keep the chain on the door, won't you?"

Belatedly I realized that she was holding

something back. "What is really bothering you, May?"

"Hilda didn't want to worry you, but a big Lincoln has been cruising by the house several times a day. Hilda is sure that it is the Rutherford car."

I tried to keep my voice steady. "It was inevitable that Max would find out about this house. Miss Miller must have Hilda's address, and Max saw us leaving the building together. He was bound to think of it sooner or later. Anyhow, he won't try to force his way in. Mr. Rutherford doesn't want any trouble — not public trouble, that is."

"Then what do you think the guy is up to? He's the one who tied you up, isn't he? — the one who gave you a beating?"

"He wants to know whether I am here. After all, he knows I had to go somewhere when I left his apartment, and he can't be sure this is the place. It's only a possibility."

"I am not going to leave you alone," May decided. "Jack would have a fit and Hilda would be really angry. She thinks a lot of you, Miss Bartlett. I can do the shopping tomorrow. Tonight we can heat up the stew we had last night. There will be enough to go round if I bake some popovers. Jack can practically eat his weight in popovers."

"Oh, let's not be silly. I'll be perfectly safe.

There's a telephone right beside the chair in the living room if I should need reinforcements."

"And you'll keep the chain on the door? Oh, dear heaven, I forgot! I can't go. There's a man coming this morning to give me an estimate on carpeting for the hall and the stairs. First impressions are so important when people look at a house, don't you think?"

"I'll be here to let him in," I reminded her.

May hovered, undecided. "Jack and Hilda will rave at me when they know I left you alone, with a strange man coming and all. Well, at least you'd be able to recognize him. He's cross-eyed."

I laughed and assured her that I would admit no one who wasn't cross-eyed.

Obediently I put the chain on the door after May had taken her reluctant departure. Then I went into the old-fashioned living room, where, from behind the lace curtains, I watched her sturdy figure walk swiftly down the street.

There wasn't much traffic, as it was a dead-end street. At the far end a moving van had drawn up to the curb, and men were lifting furniture out onto the sidewalk, unswathing the burlap wrappings and driving off a few curious children. An oil truck was parked near the corner. A small foreign car pulled away from one of the old houses, now converted into furnished rooms, and a woman went by, bundled up, her hair in rollers under a wool scarf. She was walking a dog and paused now and then, with the preoccupied expression typical of people in her position.

A taxi came up the street and the driver slowed down, looking for numbers. He stopped outside the Logan house. Instinctively I drew away from the window. Then he leaned back to open the door — as rates go up, courtesy goes down — and a stout woman, looking stouter in a thick imitation fur coat, got out and peered up at the window. It was Rose Miller.

My first reaction was one of sheer amazement at the woman's effrontery. My second was a kind of panic that, after all, an attempt was being made to get at me when I was alone in the house.

The doorbell rang and I sat still. It rang again. And again. Then Rose moved away from the door and came to look up at the windows. She stepped back as a shabby Chevrolet pulled in at the curb. The sign on the side read:

CARPETING AND DRAPERIES
NO JOB TOO BIG, NONE TOO SMALL

The driver rang the bell and I had to answer. After all, there was no possible harm Rose Miller could do me with a witness at hand.

The man at the door seemed bulky in his heavy coat and I noticed that he had crossed eyes.

"Miss Logan?"

"Miss Logan had to go out. You've come —"

"About carpeting for the stairs and hallway," he said and walked in, with Rose Miller practically treading on his heels.

"Well," she said, "so you *are* here."

"As you see."

"You go right ahead," the man said, "and I'll just look at the scene of action, so to speak, and make some measurements. I'll leave an estimate for Miss Logan. Okay?" Without waiting for any comment from me, he removed his coat and shrank from a bulky figure to a scrawny, narrow-shouldered young man. He pulled a steel tape measure, a notebook, and pencil from his pocket and began to look over the hall and the stairs, whistling tunelessly.

Rose followed me into the living room. "Mr. Rutherford wants to see you," she began abruptly. I had not asked her to sit down, but she did so. I followed suit.

"He can want," I told her. "I haven't the faintest desire to lay eyes on Mr. Rutherford ever again as long as I live."

She looked at my stick, at my bandaged ankle, at my still partly discolored eyes. "What happened to you?"

"Max happened to me," I told her.

Rose was amused. "Oh, come, Miss Weldone. I doubt very much if Max needs to beat up a woman."

"Oh, he doesn't need to; he just enjoys it. I doubt if he'd be so brave where men are concerned. He prefers picking on someone who can't fight back."

"What an outrageous —" Rose had spots of angry color burning in her cheeks, but she managed to control herself. "I didn't come here to discuss Max. I came because Mr. Rutherford is extremely anxious to talk to you. He feels that you would find it profitable to have a frank discussion with him."

"Mr. Rutherford isn't interested in profit for anyone but himself."

"Miss Weldone," Rose leaned forward, "it is quite evident to Mr. Rutherford that you and her maid Hilda were responsible for taking Mrs. Rutherford away. She is a sick woman and she should be under medical supervision. You were doing a dangerous and a cruel thing in preventing her from getting it."

"Is that what Mr. Rutherford told you?"

Rose was silent for a moment. Then she said, "You don't like Mr. Rutherford."

"You can say that again."

"He asks me to assure you that if you will cooperate with him in persuading his wife to return to him, he will compensate you in any fashion that seems fair to you. Your own terms. Those were his very words. Your own terms."

I took my time in replying. To walk straight into the spider's web with my eyes wide open would be an act of sheer imbecility. To leave myself in his hands — and in those of Max — would be to make myself a hostage and provide Rutherford with the only lever he needed to get his wife out of Philip's house.

But, I reminded myself, I wouldn't be alone with Rutherford or Max. Forrest would be there. Forrest and a whole staff of servants before whom Rutherford could ill afford a scandal. Even Rutherford must have learned that you can't bribe everyone. And if I could strike a bargain . . . I weighed the cards in my hand. I was sure Max was the blackmailer. I was sure he was the father of Mary Ann's child. I knew that Uncle

Bert's house had been bought by an Arab oil man who was one of Rutherford's business associates. I knew about the tape.

After all, it was stupid not to take the chance when I held so many trumps in my hand and so much hinged on it.

"I'll go," I told Rose.

# 15

When the carpet man left his estimate I attached a note to it, telling Hilda that I had gone with Miss Miller to the Rutherford apartment. If I were not back by eleven-thirty she was to call Lord Glydes at the Plaza, or, if she could not reach him, Mr. Philip Hanning at his brokerage office. I gave her both numbers.

There was little chance of picking up a taxi on this street, so Rose and I went to the corner, walking briskly because of the nipping wind.

"I'm surprised you came without Max and the Lincoln," I commented.

"Mr. Rutherford sent Max on an urgent errand, and he was to wait for a reply. He didn't know how long he would be." After a moment's thought Rose asked, "Why do you dislike Max so much?"

I described how Max had trailed me when I left the apartment, how he had thrown me onto the floor of the car and forced me to go to his apartment, how he had beaten and bound and gagged me, cut the telephone wire in case I got free, and took my billfold to leave me penniless.

"I don't believe it," Rose said at last.

"Didn't you learn anything about the man when you visited his apartment?" I asked.

"I've never —"

"You left a bottle of Channel Number Five there, and I remembered that you use it."

"He gave —" She broke off, flushing.

"Quite a place, isn't it?" I said. "And if you believe for one minute he furnished that from a chauffeur's salary, you are out of your mind. And while I'm about it, I'll tell you something else. He has a painting and a dressing table, both of which were stolen. He is also blackmailing Mr. Rutherford. He is dangerous, Miss Miller, very dangerous — and cruel and selfish and unscrupulous. You'd better steer clear of him. Now that Mrs. Rutherford isn't coming back, you won't have a job there anyhow."

"But she is coming back!" Rose signaled a cruising taxi and gave the driver the address of the Fifth Avenue building. As it started moving she said in a low voice, "So you did get her away. Mr. Rutherford was right."

"I helped."

"That's what Max thought."

"Mr. Rutherford was planning to have her

locked up as insane, which she is not, just as he did his daughter some months ago."

"Well, if you know what I think, he should never have let her out," Miss Miller retorted. "Look what happened when she was free. She ran off and married the first man she saw and then she killed herself."

"He wasn't the first man. The first man was Max. Under the bench of that fancy dressing table in his bedroom, the one he stole, he has a nude picture of her stepping out of his bathtub. I saw it there."

Rose Miller's lips moved soundlessly.

"And she was pregnant because of Max. If you want to know what kind of courtship she had, take a look at the bookcase in the living room of my suite — at what's hidden behind the old novels. Mary Ann could never have been unsupervised long enough to buy them for herself even if she had known what they were."

"Max didn't. He couldn't. He never loved anyone but —" She caught her breath.

"Love has nothing to do with his dealings where women are concerned."

"They chase him, you know. With his looks he can't help it. But he —"

"Save it," I said wearily. "Make a fool of yourself if you like, but Max will drop you the moment you stop being useful to him, acting as his personal spy in the Rutherford apartment. What kind of man puts a woman he cares a snap of his fingers for to doing a shabby job like that? And it isn't for Rutherford's interests. He never showed Rutherford the letter you stole from me."

"I —"

We were back on Fifth Avenue again, and the taxi driver drew up across the street from the apartment. Rose and I crossed the street together, Rose linking her arm closely with mine, as though she feared I might attempt to escape. The doorman stared when he recognized me. The guard moved nearer and then let me go past, with Rose herding me along anxiously.

The maid was waiting at the door to the apartment, so apparently the guard had informed her of our arrival. She looked after me as Rose steered me toward Mr. Rutherford's study. In answer to his summons, she opened the door, said, "Here she is, Mr. Rutherford," waited for me to go in, and then closed the door quietly behind me.

A quick glance around the room told me that Forrest was not there, and I had my first qualm. I had counted on his presence to act as a check on Rutherford. I had been relying blindly on his support. But as at least three or four people knew that I was in the apartment, I faced Rutherford with more confidence than I had expected. Nonetheless I'd have been a lot happier if I had known where Forrest was, and, above all, when he would return.

"So you decided to come back, Miss Weldone," Rutherford said. He noticed my discolored face and the stick on which I leaned. "You had better sit down."

I did so and found, to my relief, that I felt relaxed and confident.

"I understand that you arranged to have my wife leave this apartment and conveyed to the house of a total stranger rather than be put in the care of a competent physician. That is a serious action, Miss Weldone, a very serious action. If anything were to happen to her, your responsibility would be a heavy one."

"Now that she is out of your hands, nothing will happen to her," I assured him. "What do you want of me?"

"I want you to persuade my poor misguided wife to return to this apartment without any further nonsense. I want you to convince her that you are not her daughter and that you actually are Mary Ann Weldone."

"I can't do either of those things, Mr. Rutherford."

241

"I am prepared to give you my check for ten thousand dollars when my wife returns to me."

I shook my head. "I will never force her to return to you. And I told you I can't do either of the things you ask. Your wife already knows not only that I am not her daughter but that I am not" — I drew a long uncertain breath — "Mary Ann Weldone."

The heavily pouched eyes narrowed as he watched me. "What kind of game are you trying to play?" he demanded. "From the moment when you staged that meeting with my wife at Tiffany's you've been working some kind of racket. Just what is it? And who the hell are you?"

"My name is Jennifer Bartlett, and I am your son-in-law's sister."

"James Bartlett!" His hands opened and closed.

I nodded. "The man you have been trying systematically to destroy. I came here to try to put a stop to it."

"Oh, you were going to stop it." Rutherford was amused. "Your brother debauched my daughter, married her secretly knowing I would never give my consent, and then drove her to suicide — if he did not give her those sleeping pills himself."

"There's not a single word of truth in that,

Mr. Rutherford." I was surprised to find that my voice had remained calm. I wasn't even angry.

"I suppose you can prove what you are saying."

"I can tell you what I know to be the truth. Jimmy never saw your daughter until two weeks before they were married. He was not the one who got her pregnant."

"Oh, no?" Rutherford's smile was unpleasant. "She was carefully guarded from fortune hunters, Miss — Bartlett."

"Guarded by men like Max? If you want to know who debauched your daughter, look under the bench of the dressing table in Max's apartment — the dressing table he stole at your orders when he smashed the window of Jimmy's shop. And, by the way, the Sisley that caused all the scandal is in his apartment, too. You'll find a time explaining that away, Mr. Rutherford."

Rutherford brushed this aside. "What was that about looking under the bench?"

"There's a snapshot of your daughter stepping out of his bathtub. And in the sitting room of the suite I had here, behind some old romances with Mary Ann's name in them, you'll find a collection of pornography that she couldn't have bought for herself. Whose work do you suppose that was?

What kind of man deliberately corrupts a child mind?"

"Max?" He was incredulous, and then there was a startled doubt in his face.

"Max. Who else had every opportunity to meet Mary Ann? The man who was paid to keep an eye on her."

"Then why didn't he marry her?"

"He knew you wouldn't accept that, wouldn't give Mary Ann a penny. All he wanted was a hold on you."

"You are talking nonsense."

"Am I? What he was aiming for I don't know, but he got an unexpected bonus. Through Mary Ann he got a hold on you, Mr. Rutherford. How much money have you paid out already? Jimmy wasn't your blackmailer. He wouldn't stoop to such filth even if he had the information Max did. And I can tell you where a lot of your money has gone, too; into that ridiculous apartment of his, into his expensive wardrobe — there must be a dozen suits and slacks and jackets."

Rutherford came to jerk me out of my chair, grasping me by both arms. As my weight fell on my right ankle I winced.

"Max has hurt me enough. You should be satisfied with that and let me go."

For a moment his hands tightened and

then he released me. "What makes you think Max has a hold on me?"

"I assume it is that tape Mary Ann overheard."

"Your brother — I knew it."

"It wasn't Jimmy. Mary Ann never told him. She just begged him to marry her. I suppose that was because she was afraid of being sent back to Dr. Reynolds' sanitarium."

Rutherford shook his head like an enraged bull to dislodge a dart from its neck. "And the tape?"

"I assume Max has it."

There was a curious change in Rutherford's face, and I felt that somewhere I had made a misstep. Up to then I had been holding my own.

"So you think Max has this mysterious tape."

"At least he knows what is on it, and that is all that counts."

My sheer confidence did something to restore the precarious balance of forces between us. I had been wrong in thinking that Max had the tape. He simply knew of its existence. Whether Rutherford had hidden it or destroyed it did not matter much at the moment. My own impression was that if it involved a prominent man whose position was vulnerable, he would keep it as a kind of precaution.

Rutherford had worked out some plan of action that my counterattack had disturbed. For a moment he put aside the question of Max.

"What do you want of me, Miss Bartlett?"

"I want you to make a public statement, exculpating Jimmy from all the vicious charges you have brought against him. I want you to order Max to return the Sisley and make a confession that it is genuine. I want you to make him return the Queen Carlotta dressing table and compensate for the damage done to the shop and to the business and to Jimmy's reputation and his health when he was mugged by your hatchetmen. I suppose Max was one of them, too. But I can't see him tackling a man on his own. He's an awful coward, like most bullies."

I rushed on before Rutherford could comment. "I know both the Sisley and the dressing table are in Max's possession. I saw them in his apartment when he kidnapped me the night I left here. He beat me and bound me and gagged me. After you discovered that Mrs. Rutherford had escaped from you and called him, I managed to get free, but I was hurt when I had to drop off a fire escape from the second floor.

"There's a lot in that apartment to interest you, Mr. Rutherford: the furnishings that could never have been bought on the salary you'd pay a chauffeur, the snapshot of Mary Ann."

Again that confident smirk of Rutherford's. "And I suppose I'd find that mysterious tape there."

"I doubt it."

"Who told you about the alleged existence of such a tape? Your brother?"

"I told you he knew nothing about it."

"Mary Ann?"

"Mrs. Rutherford."

His face darkened. "My wife!" I saw his strong fingers curl and knew he longed to fasten them around my throat, but I knew too that he was too intelligent to make a fatal mistake.

"Mrs. Rutherford has never intended to harm you. She won't harm you now. You don't need to lock her up in a sanitarium to keep her quiet. All she wants is to be free of you, free to live her own life. She would never tell anyone what was on that tape because she has as much horror of scandal as you have, though not for the same reason. Why don't you call off your men and let her go free?"

"She's my wife," Rutherford said, "and your friend Hanning will discover that he made an expensive mistake when he interfered in my private affairs. I'll smash him and I'll smash that business of his."

"Did you ever go to a zoo and watch the javelinas?" I asked abruptly.

He was stopped short and sat gaping at me. "What the hell are you talking about?"

"They are a kind of wild pig and the silliest things I ever saw. They click their teeth together to scare each other. Sort of like the Chinese of a century ago, who went to battle wearing masks to frighten their enemies."

A reluctant grin was surprised out of Rutherford's tough face. "You're quite a girl," he said. "I wish my kid had had a quarter of your guts."

"I suppose you'd have trained her to be as crooked as you are, a kind of Fagin."

The grin faded. "Don't push your luck," Rutherford warned me. "Tell you what I'll do. I'll check on your brother and see how much truth there is in your claims about him. If they pan out as you say, I'll clear him with the press and make reasonable compensation for any trouble he has had. But I want my wife back and I want her now. Fair is fair."

"What can you do?" I asked reasonably.

"She isn't going to walk out of Philip's house of her own free will, not to come back to you. And you can't go in by force to drag her out. It's a standoff. And in time Philip's neighbors are going to wonder about the fact that there is always a car with two thugs in it sitting outside his house. They'll ask questions."

"And I can say Hanning kidnapped my wife."

"And then," I countered, "Philip will say that she is taking refuge from you. How do you want it? You aren't going to have this all your own way. And if Max isn't black-mailing you about that tape, what are you willing to bet that he won't blackmail you about your missing wife, if he should want to up the amount you are already paying him? You're going to find yourself knee-deep in scandal."

Rutherford rose from his chair, sank back again. His thick fingers drummed on the desk. "You are trying hard to throw the blame for everything onto Max, aren't you?"

"Not your treatment of Mary Ann or your wife. He's not to blame for that. But other-wise I think he is a treacherous and dan-gerous little beast," I said frankly.

He started to get up, sat down again. He

was in a state of indecision that, I thought, must be rare for him. He made a fumbling gesture. "Max double-crossing me! If that is true, it will be the first mistake I've ever made in judging a man. Why I've sent him to the post office now to . . ." His voice trailed off.

"So that's it!" I said. "You mail the black-mail money — not in cash or by check — bearer bonds, I'll bet! I suppose he'd use a different post office and a different name every time. That's what Max is supposed to be doing now: waiting at the post office for the man to pick up the envelope, so that he can catch him in the act. You know, Mr. Rutherford, you really are an easy mark."

"Not many people would agree with you."

"That Chinese army afraid of each other's masks? Well, I'll bet anything you like that Max never mailed those envelopes and that the bearer bonds are in a safety deposit box right now."

Rutherford pushed back his chair with a violent gesture. "Okay, we'll clear this up at any rate. Come along."

I clung to the arm of my chair. "Come where?"

"I'm going to Max's apartment to see for myself and you are coming with me."

"I'm not going."

"Come on. I have no time to waste."

"*I'm not going.* Try to make me and I'll scream."

"The girl who came under a false name with false references and tried to convince my poor misled wife that she was our dead daughter. A girl who came here today to blackmail me, as her brother has been doing. My word against yours. Your word against the stories that appeared in the press about your brother. You go right ahead and scream." He was smiling now. "I'm calling you, sister. Show your hole card."

But I didn't have one now. I'd played out all my hand. Why didn't Forrest come? Where was the big oaf at a time when I needed him so terribly? To go to Max's apartment, to face him and Rutherford together, defenseless . . . No, I couldn't do it.

"I want to make a telephone call first."

He laughed aloud at that. "I couldn't be less surprised. Not a chance. Are you coming?"

I got to my feet without further resistance. We went down in the elevator together and the doorman rushed to signal for a cab and helped us in with tender care. We rode in silence, Rutherford plunged in thought.

Abruptly he asked, "What's in this for you?"

"I want the persecution of my brother stopped."

"And your interference with my wife?"

"I was just terribly sorry for her, and I knew if you succeeded in getting her locked up she might crack mentally. I couldn't stand by and let that happen."

He thought it over. Then he said, "You and your brother have caused me a lot of trouble, Miss Bartlett."

"Jimmy was as much a victim as Mary Ann. She was the one who wanted him to marry her. She knew she was pregnant and she was scared stiff — scared of Max and scared of you. The poor thing didn't know what to do. She couldn't take it. I guess she just couldn't take anything."

"Where did she get those sleeping pills?"

"She stole them from her mother, who had collected them to kill herself rather than go on living with you."

That stopped him cold — for the moment, at least.

When Rutherford had paid off the driver we went into the building and he verified Max's name over a mailbox. We went up the uncarpeted stairs, making what seemed to me a great deal of noise because today there was no din of rock and roll from the top floor.

"This is the apartment," I said, "but . . ."

"But what?"

"Max must be in there." Instinctively I stepped back. "There should be a padlock and it's gone."

For a moment Rutherford hesitated. Then he slid his hand into his overcoat pocket and brought out a small revolver. He reached past me and turned the knob gently and then pushed the door open. With his body behind me, shoving, I went first into the room, Rutherford close behind, using me as a shield. The gallant type, Mr. Rutherford. The living room was empty, but someone was moving around in the bedroom.

Rutherford, still using me as a shield, crossed the room swiftly and threw open the door. The man who turned away from the open drawer of the dressing table was Forrest Preston.

# 16

It was like one of those television movie endings with the final tableau frozen on the screen. The three of us simply stared at each other, all equally taken aback. Rutherford recovered first.

"What the hell," he exploded, "are you doing here?"

Forrest only briefly glanced at the revolver in Rutherford's hand, observed that I was being used as a cover. His voice was, as usual, somewhat bored and without any excitement.

"You gave me a rather pressing assignment, sir," he said, looking at Rutherford, "and I came here to check out a possibility."

"You think Max is . . ." Rutherford hesitated.

"It appears to be a possibility — more than a possibility. With his opportunities it seems almost inevitable he is the man you have been looking for." Forrest was in complete control of himself, an earnest young man wholly absorbed in doing his duty and rather modestly proud of having brought off a clever coup. But I knew that his attention never wavered from the revolver in Rutherford's hand and the fact that I stood between the two men. He was on thin ice and keenly aware of it.

"Have you found anything?"

Before Forrest could answer, I said, "In the living room is the Sisley that caused such a scandal for Jimmy, and that dressing table was stolen from our display window."

Forrest looked at me sharply at that. So I had revealed my true identity to Rutherford. I could see him struggling to get his bearings, not certain how much I had told, how much I might have been forced to tell. The very fact that I was there in Rutherford's company, being used as a shield, was enough to keep him on the alert.

I half turned to Rutherford. "You promised me! You said you'd clear Jimmy if I gave you some evidence of Max's complicity, his relations with Mary Ann, and his heavy expenditures that would have been impossible on his salary."

"Okay." Rutherford brushed this aside. "That can wait." Jimmy and I were of little account at the moment. He turned back to Forrest.

Again before Forrest could speak I said, "Look under the dressing table bench.

You'll find a snapshot."

Forrest turned the bench over and Rutherford lunged toward it, jerked off the snapshot, his face suffused with an ugly red. Even then, I think, it was not the outrage done his daughter, who was incompetent to look after herself; it was the humiliating factor of having been double-crossed by his henchman that infuriated him.

He started to rip the snapshot and then put it in his billfold. "I'll kill him for this," he said. He had shifted the revolver to his other hand and was holding it carelessly.

"Careful, sir. You don't want that to go off."

"It won't." Rutherford dropped it back in his pocket. "What put you on to Max?"

"It's hard to tell. Little things. I had learned, for instance, that he was using one of the women on your staff to search the apartment. He picked up the mail every day and turned over only what he wanted you to see."

"Who was the woman?"

I made a half-protesting sound, but Forrest ignored me. "It was Rose Miller," he said coolly.

"Miller?" Rutherford said blankly. "Sarah's secretary?" He added in surprise, "She had a good job here. Why did she take a chance on losing it and getting thrown out without a recommendation? And believe me that is what is going to happen to her."

"Well, there were big stakes for her. A middle-aged woman's last chance at romance." Forrest saw how angry I was, but he continued to ignore me.

"You've got nothing but a lot of theory," Rutherford said impatiently. "I want facts. If necessary I'll break Max so he'll never lift a finger again, but I want facts. I have to know what he knows."

"The furnishings in this apartment are facts. The wardrobe in that closet is a fact. Max has been getting money from somewhere — a lot of money."

"You didn't find any bearer bonds?"

"Bearer bonds. Is that how —" Forrest checked himself. "No, nothing like that. No money in the place. No checkbook. No key to a safety deposit box. He probably carries that on him. No letters or documents of any kind."

Rutherford did not inquire whether he had come across an unidentified tape, and that added to my conviction that he either had the tape in his possession or he had destroyed it.

"Then I guess there is nothing further to be done here." Rutherford took a hasty look around. "All right, let's go."

I tugged at his arm. "And the Sisley? And the dressing table?"

"You really are a little fighter. I'll see that they are returned to your brother's shop," Rutherford assured me, "but not until you have done a little restoration of your own, Miss Bartlett."

Forrest's eyes flickered at that. Casual and elegant and relaxed, he had been behaving with that air of boredom that was so infuriating. He had not seemed to look at me at all. I had been leaning against the wall to take some of the weight off my sprained ankle, because standing was too painful. Now he stretched out long fingers, touched my arm, pushed me onto the dressing table bench. "You'd better sit down, hadn't you? And when we leave here? I'll see that you get home. You don't look very fit." So he was trying to take care of me, to get me out of Rutherford's hands.

The latter said, "Not so fast, Forrest. She and I have a little unfinished business."

Someone ran up the stairs and stopped abruptly outside the open door of the apartment. Forrest turned like a well-oiled machine. Then footsteps crossed the living room rapidly, almost at a run, and Max stood in the doorway, trim in his uniform, as handsome as ever, impassive even in the face of this unexpected invasion. Only his eyes were wildly alive.

He looked from me to Forrest to Rutherford. Paused there. "Mr. Rutherford! What —"

"We just came around to ask you a few questions, Max," Rutherford said.

Max swallowed. He hadn't been prepared for this, not for Forrest, certainly not for me, absolutely not for Rutherford. "All you needed was to give me a call, sir."

"Any luck at the post office, Max?" Rutherford was at his blandest.

"Sorry, sir. I was watching the whole time. No man named Harry Brooks picked up a big green envelope at general delivery."

"I couldn't be less surprised." Rutherford was at his most jovial. "What never went into the mail wouldn't come out of it."

"What —" Max's ruddy color was fading.

"We've been admiring your apartment, Max. Very nice indeed. Quite a wardrobe you have. On your salary you must be a real bargain hunter to get such results. Oh, by the way, the painting and the dressing table are to be returned to Mr. Bartlett's shop within twenty-four hours."

"But I was only carrying out orders!"

"This is an order, Max."

"It would be interesting," Forrest drawled in his lazy voice, "to know whether Max has a long green envelope in his pocket, or at least a key to a safety deposit box."

That was when Max knew that the game was up. And no one knew better than he just how powerful an opponent he had in his boss. He moved so quickly that none of us were prepared, jerked me off the bench in front of him, and had a revolver in his hand. Rutherford drew his and Max said softly, "You'll hit her, you know."

"For God's sake, Max!" Forrest exclaimed. "The game is up. Let the girl go. You'll only do yourself more harm."

"Yes? She is my bargaining point." Max started backing slowly toward the door with me a helpless shield in front of him. Like master like man. "One shot and I'll kill her. Make no mistake about that. I owe her a lot already," and he twisted my arm so that I whimpered.

Forrest waited, white-faced, helpless, while Max continued his slow progress toward the door. Once outside, he dragged me headlong down the stairs and out to the curb, where he hurled me into the back of the Lincoln. Doors slammed, the motor raced, and we were off.

Apparently Rutherford followed us, because there was a shot at the tires and Max laughed softly. I had landed on my right side and nearly blacked out with pain. But this time, this time, I told myself fiercely, Forrest knew what had happened. Forrest would help me.

This time I did not attempt to get up or to open the door. I knew it would be no use. What was going to happen to me? Max had lost his racket as well as his job and his easy income. He had also lost the possessions in which he took such pride. Now that he had been exposed, he could no longer blackmail Rutherford. Whatever he knew, however damaging it might be, it was worthless in his hands. Of course he must have a lot of money cached away somewhere, but while he was on the run it would be difficult to get at it. Within hours his picture would be circulated in every bank in the city. His name would not matter — it was highly unlikely that he would rent a safety deposit box under his own name. But he could not conceal those spectacular good looks.

Where could he go? What could he do? And what was he going to do with me? Dead, I told myself, I would only be an additional risk to him. He couldn't intend to kill me. But when and how would he release me? One thing was sure. He dared not go far in the Lincoln. The number would be in the hands of the police within minutes, if indeed Forrest had not already taken care of that.

Apparently Max, too, was at a loss as to his next move. He drove aimlessly through Central Park, apparently weighing various possibilities, and once I heard him cursing in a low voice — a long vicious stream of profanity. Whatever was going to happen, and happen soon, I was going to have to suffer for my part in Max's exposure.

Then the car stopped, turned, and headed back across the park, this time at a faster pace. At last Max had determined on a destination. We went down a short incline and the car slid into its slot. Max had returned it to Rutherford's underground parking garage across the street from his own apartment. Surely he was not going back there! By this time Rutherford or Forrest had undoubtedly alerted the police, who would be in charge.

He got out from under the wheel, opened the back door, and, as before, jerked me out of the car, but this time I had a sprained ankle and cracked ribs. I smothered a yell, knowing instinctively that this was no time to attract any attention. Max still had a revolver and he had me as a target.

"Walk," he said, and we went up the incline. "Don't look across the street or make the slightest disturbance to attract attention. Believe me, it's the last thing you will ever do."

I could not help giving a quick look across the street. A police car was parked outside Max's apartment building, but it was empty. The men must have gone upstairs.

Max laughed softly. "Walk," he said again.

"It hurts without a stick."

"You'll hurt worse before we are done," he promised me. "At this point I have nothing to lose, thanks chiefly to you, so watch your step. I mean that. It's only five blocks. That won't kill you." Not, he made clear, that he would care if it did.

Five blocks. It dawned on me that we were going back to the Rutherford apartment, which was tantamount to walking straight into the lion's den. I raised incredulous eyes to his face. "You're out of your mind." I stumbled over a curb.

He held me upright. "Keep walking."

"But Rutherford's —"

"Where else? Until I can make some arrangements. We can't take a cab or any kind of public transportation. Your eyes are conspicuous and, well, so am I."

I found myself grinning and then wished I

263

hadn't. Max's colossal vanity could not endure mockery.

"We can't hire a room anywhere," Max went on thinking aloud, "because we have no luggage, and we'll be hunted before long. No, when I get out on the street again, I want guaranteed safe conduct."

"And you think you'll get it?"

"I know I will. The police aren't going to risk a woman's life even on Rutherford's say-so. How much did you tell him?"

"He knows I am Jimmy Bartlett's sister —"

"For God's sake!"

"— and that you are the father of Mary Ann's child and his blackmailer."

Max's fingers dug into an arm muscle, so that it was all I could do not to cry out. I think I would have if I had not seen how avidly he watched me, tasting my pain. "I wish I'd killed you when I had you in my apartment before. How did you get away?"

"Wouldn't you like to know?"

"Don't be funny with me. Does Rutherford know you helped his wife get away?"

"Yes."

"You sure are the spanner in the works. Now, quick while there's no traffic on the street," and he pulled me inside the service entrance to the Rutherford building. He was

264

as wary now as a wild animal, looking around him, listening, his very nose seeming to quiver as it searched the air for danger.

Keeping me in front of him, his revolver in his right hand, he went to the service elevator, saw that the door was open, and shoved me in. We began the long slow ride to the twelfth floor.

When the elevator came to a halt, Max looked carefully around and then pushed me out ahead of him. Noiselessly he turned the knob of the kitchen door, which held. He put his ear against the panel, listening. Apparently there were no sounds in the kitchen, and he drew out a key ring, fitted a key into the lock — I should have realized, I thought numbly, that he would have had time while he worked for Rutherford to get duplicate keys to all the doors — and eased the door open, pushing me ahead of him.

We went up the service stairs at the back of the apartment as silently as ghosts, past the second floor, to the third. But it was not to my unoccupied suite he drove me, but to Rose Miller's. He eased that door open and then shoved me inside, following like a ghost and closing the door behind us.

Rose had been sitting at her desk, before her typewriter, looking emptily ahead of her. She looked up, gasped, and then sat staring as the full meaning of the picture struck her. Max holding me as a shield in front of him, a revolver in his right hand.

"Max!"

"Quiet," he said.

"Max?" It was a terrible question. And then she relaxed. "Oh, wonderful! You've made her come back here to force Mrs. Rutherford to come home. You'll get a bonus for this, see if you don't. You are really wonderful."

"Now that," he said softly, "is really an idea. You've got a head on your shoulders, Beautiful. Together we can go places."

She glowed.

Max turned to me. "All right, Jennifer baby. Rutherford is going to make some big allowances if his wife is returned to him. You are going to get hold of this guy Hanning and say that unless Mrs. Rutherford is returned here within one hour you are going to die." He gestured toward the telephone on Rose's desk. "Go ahead, Jennifer. Time's a-wasting."

"Rose," I said desperately, "Max has kidnapped me. Do you understand what that means? If you become an accessory, you will get a life term in prison. No deal will help you. And Max will let you take the rap alone. He's the kind of man who uses women as a shield, as he has been using me, hiding behind me. That's Max."

Max struck me across the face so viciously that I fell backwards and toppled over the arm of a chair, striking my taped ribs. He leaped toward me and covered my mouth with his hand to stifle any sound of pain. I stared at Rose. Surely she must understand how ruthless, how brutal the man was.

She was staggered all right, but she turned from me to Max, a question in her eyes, as the sunflower turns to its god as it sets. No help there. She might have no illusions, but she was as hopelessly hooked as if she were on hard drugs.

The telephone on Rose's desk rang and we all jumped at the unexpected sound. Rose reached for it with a shaking hand. "Miss Miller speaking," she said. She listened. "Mr. Rutherford is not here. Neither is his assistant. You might try the downtown office. . . . Who? Mr. Logan? Does he have an appointment? . . . Sorry, but I have no authority to admit anyone in Mr. Rutherford's absence. I am his wife's secretary, not his. I —"

I jerked away from Max's restraining hand and shouted, "Tell him to come up! Tell him — Help!" I shouted at the top of my voice, hoping that Big Jack would hear my voice if he was standing near the house phone in the lobby.

There was a confusion of sound and Big Jack yelled, "Okay. I'm on my way."

As Max lunged for me, his face congested with fury, I laughed exultantly. "You'd better get out while you can. That's Big Jack Logan, the boxer, and he is simply itching to get his hands on you. Oh" — as he raised the revolver — "don't wave that thing around. You're stuck here. It won't do you a scrap of good to add murder to kidnapping and robbery and all the rest of it, including blackmail. You'd better run while you still can."

I think that was the hardest thing Max ever did. He wanted in the worst way to wring my neck or at least to beat me up, but time was against him. At the last moment fury overcame him. He jerked me off the chair arm onto the floor, kicked me brutally in the ribs, and then he was gone, running down the hall towards the servants' stairs.

"Max," Rose cried, "Max, wait for me!" She ran out of the room, down the hall. "Max!" Down below a door slammed. There was an altercation at the front door, and then Big Jack was shouting, "Miss Bartlett! Are you there?"

"Here." I picked myself off the floor and

began making my way painfully toward the front stairs, grasping the bannister for support. I started slowly down, reached the second floor and started down the last flight. Big Jack saw me and came leaping up toward me, followed by the shouts of the servants, who had been alerted from the downstairs lobby. A man whom I recognized as the armed guard shouted, "Stop, or I'll fire!"

I don't think Jack even heard him. He came up those stairs like a rocket. "Where is he?"

"He got away. Out the service entrance."

And then the guard was beside us, his hand on Jack's arm. The latter turned to him and said mildly, "You're after the wrong guy, mister. The one you want is Rutherford's chauffeur, a wart of a man, who kidnapped this lady and, from the looks of things, beat her up again. You all right, Miss Bartlett?"

I nodded. "How did you find me?"

He grinned. "Your friend Tom O'Connor saw the getaway in the Lincoln and saw someone shoot at the tires."

"That was Mr. Rutherford."

"Well, Tom called me at the number you had given him. May had come home and found you gone, and she and Hilda are just about going out of their minds. So I got myself up to the chauffeur's apartment just in time to see him return and park the car. I couldn't figure out what gave. I could see a police car across the street. Then Max came up the incline pulling you along and set off for this place. I'd have taken him then and there if it hadn't been for that revolver. I knew he'd get you first."

"I've never in all my life been so glad to see anyone," I told him fervently. "You know what? I think you're beautiful."

He grinned. "I've been called a lot of things, but that is the first time for that."

The guard had sheathed his revolver and was standing at a loss when the outside door opened and Rutherford and Forrest came in.

Everyone seemed to speak at once. The maid at the door and the guard both attempted to explain how Big Jack Logan had forced his way into the apartment. Rutherford was demanding, "Where is Max?" And Forrest came to me saying, "Jennifer! Are you all right? Oh God, are you all right?"

"You can see she's not all right," Jack said. "And now, if you'll all get out of the way, I'm taking her back to my house, where she will be safe. She sure as hell isn't safe here."

"Not quite yet, mister," Rutherford said. "We have some unfinished business, Miss Bartlett and I."

# 17

To my surprise Forrest made a muttered excuse and went quickly down to the study, closing the door. I looked after him blankly. It was impossible that he would do this to me, simply turn his back and leave me in Rutherford's hands.

Rutherford turned to his guard. "Get this man out of here," indicating Jack. "He forced his way into my apartment. That's what you are paid for, and so far I haven't known any way in which you earn your living. You let Mrs. Rutherford walk out. You let this guy walk in."

"I'm not leaving without the lady," Jack told him. "She was kidnapped and brought here by force. You can see for yourselves the shape she is in. Rutherford's chauffeur got her, but he has managed to escape."

"Yeah." Rutherford's eyes were on the hapless guard again. "You let him get away."

"He never came past me," the poor man said. "Anyhow, no one told me he wasn't one of your most trusted employees, as I had understood. How am I supposed to know these things? By radar?"

"Impertinence on top of incompetence. This is the last confidential job you'll ever hold for anyone. I'll see to that. Now get out and take that fellow with you."

The guard looked dubiously at Jack, who grinned amiably at him. "You'd have to shoot me to get me out of here without the lady," he said.

"You're Big Jack Logan?"

"That's right."

"Then you're straight. I'm not making trouble for straight guys." The guard hesitated and then gulped and said, "Sorry, Mr. Rutherford, but I'm giving up the job."

"Giving it up? You're fired!"

The guard shrugged and went out. Jack leaned against a table and waited. He wasn't hostile, simply immovable.

And then Forrest came back. "Oh," Rutherford said with elaborate politeness, "so you have decided to return. I thought perhaps you had simply walked out, like my guard."

"And Max."

As Rutherford's face began to swell, Forrest went on unhurriedly, "I've amplified that report to the police we made from Max's apartment. They are going to check banks. I wish we had a picture of him to circulate. That would be the quickest way."

"I'll bet anything that Rose Miller has a picture of him," I said. "He's the kind to have as many photographs taken as a movie star."

Forrest went up the stairs and came back in a few minutes with Rose, her face swollen and blotched from crying. He helped her gently into a chair. "We just want some information, Miss Miller. The police are going to pick up Max, who is wanted for kidnapping, blackmail, breaking and entering, probably a mugging charge. He's facing a long stretch in prison and, as long as he is free, he is dangerous. For the safety of everyone, he must be captured as quickly as possible. We need a picture of him to circulate. Have you —"

She shook her head.

"Rose," I said, "he walked out on you as I told you he would. He's brutal and evil. Please help us stop him. Please!" As she was silent, lips set stubbornly, I said, "That elaborate apartment was paid for by blackmail. So was his wardrobe. And you saw for yourself that he used my body as a shield to protect him from a man. He's a coward, Rose, a treacherous coward. No good to you. No good to anyone. A man who could seduce a helpless girl like Mary Ann just to get hold on her father."

She looked at me then. No one spoke or moved. Then she got up slowly and started for the stairs. As Forrest put out a hand to stop her I made a desperate gesture, and his hand dropped. With flagging steps, she went up the stairs along to her room. Then there was silence. Forrest moved and I shook my head violently. At last her door opened and she returned, a big cabinet picture in her hand. She came down the stairs, gave it to Forrest, and then went back to her room, climbing as though the stairs were endless.

Forrest went into the study and returned to say, "I've called the police. A man will be here to pick this up and have copies made to distribute to airports, banks, bus terminals. Max can't get far without money or a change from that conspicuous chauffeur's uniform, and he can't go back to his apartment because there's a man from the police inside."

Rutherford was certainly a man with one idea. None of this seemed to make any impression on him. "And now, Miss Bartlett," he said, "I want to talk to you about my wife. You accuse Max of kidnapping. In removing my wife from under my roof to that of a stranger you, too, are guilty of kidnapping. You are also preventing her from being put in the hands of a physician whose help she desperately needs. These are criminal actions."

Jack stirred and then was silent, leaning back against the table. The servants had left, after a gesture from Rutherford.

"Actually," I said, trying to forget how my side felt after Max's kick, "it isn't I holding your wife prisoner in Philip Hanning's house; it is your own men. I think the police would take a different view from yours about her captivity if they were called in."

"I am still her husband, Miss Bartlett. I have certain rights. The police won't question them."

"She has rights, too."

The telephone rang and Forrest went in to answer it. He was gone for some time.

"Just what do you want me to do?" I asked.

"I want you to persuade my wife to return to me without occasioning any public comment or scandal. If she is so bitterly opposed to Dr. Reynolds, though that is a totally irrational attitude, I'll yield to her demands, no matter how absurd they may be. No one can say I am an unreasonable man. Tell her that, will you? Say that if she will come back I will make no further request that she receive medical attention. That is a promise."

The maid who answered the door came in to say, "There's a man here, sir, from the police." Her eyes were wide with excitement. Heaven knows what rumors were circulating among the staff, what with Max's escape, Jack's noisy arrival, and now the police.

"Bring him in."

As the man in plainclothes came into the room, Forrest returned from the study. "This is what you want," he said and held out the photograph. I couldn't resist taking a peek at it. As I might have expected it was colored.

The policeman nodded. "Can you answer a few questions?" Forrest gave him Max's name, address, age, and explained that he was wanted for kidnapping, blackmail, and probably theft. At least those would do for a start. "And," he concluded, "he is armed and desperate. He had to leave without having an opportunity to get his hands on any money, so you'd better be alerted for a holdup job. He must have safety deposit boxes somewhere and probably checking accounts. Get copies of the picture to banks as fast as possible."

The plainclothesman nodded, took a long thoughtful look at Rutherford, a look of surprised recognition at Logan, and then he was gone. Not a man to waste time.

The telephone in the study rang again, and once more Forrest went in to answer it. When he returned Rutherford was saying, "I'm tired of horsing around. Get on the phone at Hanning's house and talk to my wife, Miss Bartlett."

"There's not much point in that," Forrest said. "Mrs. Rutherford isn't there."

Rutherford smiled. "She couldn't get away. I have two men watching the house at all times."

"You *had* two men," Forrest said gently. "The siege was lifted twenty minutes ago, when your men were taken away."

"What do you mean — taken away? Who took them?"

"Uncle Sam," Forrest said pleasantly.

"What the hell are you getting at? If you've been double-crossing me, I'll crucify you."

"As an expert in the art of double-crossing," Forrest said, "you ought to know more about it than I do. I've been here, assigned by the government, which takes considerable interest in you, Mr. Rutherford. It has given you a lot of rope, so far, but it doesn't hold with keeping a wife captive. Some of the Treasury boys picked up your goons and put them under arrest. Another of them escorted your wife to the airport, where she should be embarking for Reno in another hour and a half. She isn't coming back to you ever, Mr. Rutherford. Never again. But she won't betray you unless you force her to do so."

"Good God, she can't divorce me now, just when I'm to be made ambassador to the Court of St. James. They don't approve of divorce."

Forrest shrugged.

All this time Logan hadn't moved, his eyes bright with excitement, taking in all that was happening. He was accustomed to a world in which battles were fought with fists, not with words.

"What's in this for you, Forrest?" Rutherford asked. "As I told you before, I'm a reasonable man."

"I'm part of a task force that has been working ever since Watergate — and that should have been working long before that. We're trying to unearth crookedness, to expose the men who exploit America, to prevent any conspiracy from getting into its stride."

"But why pick on me?"

"That's their decision. I might tell you that there is a small army of men going over the books of your interlocking companies,

Mr. Rutherford. Already they have made some startling discoveries, and they are only at the beginning. You must have kept some of that stuff aloft by sheer sleight of hand, but when it begins to slip —" Forrest shook his head.

Rutherford had dropped into a chair. He rang a bell on the table and said sharply to the maid who answered, "Scotch." Then he made a vague circular gesture that indicated us all.

Jack shook his head. "Not for me. Milk, if you have it."

"Dry sherry," I said.

"Scotch," Forrest said.

"Why me?" Rutherford asked when the maid had gone. "Why me? You think every businessman except me is lily white? For that matter, do you think labor leaders are lily white? They do their share to fill up our prisons."

"The American people are getting sick and tired of being cheated, whoever does it, whether industrialists or labor or doctors or lawyers or thieves or whatever. Clean government is possible when the people want it enough to fight for it. And it doesn't take many. We are putting you and other men like you out of business, Rutherford. You aren't going to have things your own way any longer. You aren't going to conceal your crooked business dealings. You aren't going to have uncontested power. And you are going to pay your taxes."

"So." There was a pause. Then Rutherford smiled. "And, of course, you have evidence that I don't pay my taxes." He saw Forrest's expression and his smile deepened. "Just what are you going to tell the court, Forrest? Where are the nice facts you are going to hand them? You can have a dozen men or a hundred men going over the books of my companies, but you won't find that there is any evidence that taxes aren't paid."

"We'll find it," Forrest said.

The maid came in with a tray and distributed the glasses. When she had gone Rutherford lifted his to his lips and drank deeply. There was a slight tremor in his fingers when he set the glass down on the table. He looked at Forrest.

"Your work here is done," he said. "You can hardly expect me to pay you a salary in order to spy on me."

Forrest didn't like that. I could see the color rising under his skin. Rutherford saw it, too.

"Spying," he repeated. "Not a nice word for a man stuffed with such virtuous ideas, is it?"

"A prison guard has an unpleasant job," Forrest said quietly, "but it is made necessary by the criminals whom he has to keep in order."

"And how much have you learned about me? I'm sure you'd like all this to be open and aboveboard, just for a change?"

Another flick of the whip that Forrest felt.

"Well, as I said, we have a small army checking on your interlocking businesses. We know of your dealings with at least one Arab oil man — the one who bought Lord Glydes' estate — though you've been bellowing about protecting the rights of the American oil companies. And, incidentally, Lord Glydes regards you as a most unsavory crook and is devoting himself to the effort to prevent your appointment being approved for the ambassadorship. He feels Britain and America can understand each other better without men of your caliber to gum up the works."

At Rutherford's expression, Logan stirred and then was still again.

"And, of course," Forrest went on tranquilly, "we know of the existence of the tape on which you discussed with a man in high position the operation by which you were moving large blocks of money into numbered Swiss accounts. When we have that tape . . ."

Once more Rutherford smiled. He held the trump card and he knew it.

"Go ahead," he said, "but get out of this apartment now, Forrest. Now!"

Forrest got up and went to the door. "In here, please," he said, and two men came into the room. "Show Mr. Rutherford your search warrant."

One of them did so.

"Now go ahead. You know what you are looking for. A tape. It may be put with a collection of tapes and with a misleading title. It may be anywhere."

Rutherford drained his glass and sat drumming his thick fingers on the table. "You're going to regret this, Forrest. My God, how you are going to regret this." He had somehow regained his air of invincibility, that aura of power that was so dangerous because people believe in it.

He reached in a coat pocket and Forrest, remembering the revolver, was alert at once. Instead, Rutherford pulled out a heavily carved Dutch pipe and a pocket knife. He pulled an ashtray from the table closer to him, and with his knife he cleaned the bowl of the pipe, apparently concentrating on the task, forgetting our existence. Then he reached for the beautiful cloisonné tobacco jar, lifted off the top, and began to fill the pipe, pressing down the tobacco.

Jack moved like a coiled spring, his big hand clamped over Rutherford's wrist. "Hold it!" he snapped.

Rutherford gaped at him, trying to free his hand. Jack increased his pressure and the fingers opened. Jack reached into the jar and pulled out the object Rutherford had dropped.

"I guess this is the tape you were looking for."

"Well, for God's sake," Forrest exclaimed. "How did you do it?"

"Well, I'm not up to this fancy talk, but I'm trained to watch hands," Jack explained.

Forrest took the tape from him and stood turning it over and over. "Such a little thing to cause so much trouble. I'll call off the search." He started for the stairs and I sat looking after him, feeling limp now that the search was over, now that Mrs. Rutherford was free, now that Jimmy would be cleared. My job was done and I was almost too tired to care.

And then I saw the revolver in Rutherford's hand, heard the report, and smelled the powder. Numbly I realized that I was unhurt and then I saw Rutherford's head — what had been his head — and I screamed.

# 18

The room was filled with people: the two policemen; half a dozen servants; Forrest, who came leaping back down the stairs. There were shouts, questions, an hysterical scream from one of the maids. Only Logan and I — and Mr. Rutherford — were motionless.

Then, with Forrest's help, the police restored order, drove out the servants, and while one of the men called the precinct for men and equipment, the other stood looking down at Rutherford, the revolver still clutched in his hand, and that hideous hole in his head.

"Why now?" he asked. "What triggered this?"

"Everything fell on him at once," Forrest answered. "He discovered that his goons had been removed from the Hanning house by the FBI and that his wife had got away and was heading for Reno. He knew the Treasury boys were digging into his business deals. He discovered that he was not going to get his appointment confirmed as ambassador to Great Britain. And then we found this." He opened his hand and displayed the tape.

"What's on it?"

Forrest shrugged. "I haven't heard the thing. According to Mrs. Rutherford, it contains a discussion with a 'man in high place' about the process of unloading large amounts of money in Swiss numbered accounts. Dynamite because it means both men were falsifying their tax returns."

"And you found it?"

Forrest indicated Jack. "He did. He was watching Rutherford's hands and saw him drop the thing into the tobacco jar."

"You'd better hand it over," the policeman suggested and Forrest did so, rather reluctantly, I thought.

"I don't suppose," he said wryly, "I'll ever hear that tape."

"Depends on what it contains," the other replied. "If it involves a big shot — someone high up in government circles or in industry — it would be top secret, and I guess it was that, to drive the guy to kill himself. This is out of the hands of the police. It's the Treasury's baby."

And then a small group of men entered the room, quiet, efficient, taking over. When we had identified ourselves, we were asked to go into another room, which, at Forrest's

might call that kid Tom O'Connor who got the word to you. We owe him that much. Tell him — well, tell him he saved the girl. He'd like that. See you."

When the policeman had left, I looked at Jack and said soberly, "You said you had learned to watch hands. You knew what he was going to do. You could have stopped him."

"Well, the way I look at it, Miss Bartlett, is that any adult in his right mind has a right to dispose of his own body the way he wants. Anyhow, this guy was all washed up. People like that, you destroy their confidence and they're licked right there. You see it over and over in the ring. You've got to have confidence. And it costs a lot to keep some of these guys alive for the rest of their time at the public expense. Saves everyone a lot of misery, and I guess his wife had a break coming to her."

The policeman was back again, reaching for the telephone. Jack and I did not pretend not to be listening. Then we realized that he was calling La Guardia to have the man escorting Mrs. Rutherford paged. He was to bring her back to the apartment.

"Oh, no," I cried when he had set down the telephone. "She's had enough. If she sees him like that —"

"She won't. We'll have him out of here in another half hour — just as soon as we can get some pictures and drawings."

"But —"

"Look, miss," the policeman said reasonably, "she don't need a divorce now, see?"

"May I make a call?"

He nodded but waited to supervise and prevent me from being indiscreet. Only afterwards did it occur to me that he suspected I might be calling the news media to give them an exclusive and get myself a publicity break.

It was Jimmy who answered Philip's phone. "Jen! What gives? The goons staked out in front of the house have been called off and Mrs. Rutherford got away, headed for Reno, with a government escort to make sure she gets there. I couldn't reach you at that house in the Bronx. I just got hold of a couple of women acting half crazy and saying you'd been kidnapped again."

"I was, but I'm all right."

"Where are you?"

"The Rutherford apartment."

"Rutherford!" He shouted so loud that I held the receiver away from my ear.

"He's dead," I said. "He shot himself. And the police are here. . . . No, of course, I'm not in trouble. . . . I don't know just when I'll be able to leave here. . . . Yes, I knew Mrs. Rutherford got away. They are going to bring her back from the airport. . . . Well, she doesn't need a divorce now, you see. . . . Where? At the shop? Oh, fine!" Then I wailed, "Oh, Jimmy, I didn't get back the Sisley or the Queen Carlotta dressing table. Mr. Rutherford promised to make Max return them today, but he has disappeared. And now Mr. Rutherford is dead and he can never clear you. . . . Yes, it does too matter. It matters terribly. . . . All right, I'll see you at the shop. . . . What? . . . No, I don't need Philip. I'm quite all right."

And then a plainclothes detective, accompanied by a young policeman, came in and asked Jack to go out. He settled himself in Rutherford's chair, and the policeman drew out a notebook. I told them everything I knew, and when I had finished we started all over again and I told him things I had forgotten. Now and then he looked at me with astonished eyes, but for the most part he prodded for more information.

"Well," he said at last, and there was a flicker of amusement at the corner of his lips, a glint of laughter in his eyes, "you seem to have been a busy young lady. We could use you on the force. You've cleared up the mystery of Mary Ann Rutherford's suicide. You discovered the existence of the tape that led to Rutherford's death. You got Mrs. Rutherford away from her husband and Dr. Reynolds. We've had rumors about that place of his in Westchester before now."

"But I failed in the one thing I set out to do, clear my brother."

The detective grinned at me. "I think Mrs. Rutherford will be glad to do that for you. She owes you quite a lot, it seems to me."

"Will the true story about her daughter have to come out? She's had so much unhappiness without all that being dragged into the public eye. She deserves some privacy."

"It will be all right, miss. The police have sat on a lot of information that was more important than that. Well, I guess you've helped us clear up a lot of loose ends."

I shook my head. "Nothing is finished in this case as long as Max is free. I'll never draw an easy breath while he is free. He is dangerous, really dangerous. He hurts people because he likes doing it."

"You can relax. We'll pick him up."

"How?"

"He hasn't any money. He is wearing a uniform that is easily identifiable. And, according to what I've heard from the women around here — and what's wrong with that Miller woman? — he is a startlingly handsome guy."

"Poor Rose Miller! What will happen to her? She fell head over heels in love with him; she did anything he asked of her; and now, when she was ready and willing to help him, he walked out on her. The humiliation — that is what is really going to grind into her flesh; having been rejected."

"She was aiding and abetting in a kidnapping," the detective reminded me, unmoved by my plea.

"But she didn't really do anything. Jack came before she could."

"And if he hadn't come?" When I was silent he said, "You can't afford to be sentimental about people who perform criminal actions, Miss Bartlett. How would you feel if it had been someone else Max had kidnapped — someone you loved — and your friend Miss Miller was helping him?"

I had no answer to that.

"All right, you can go now. No use in you hanging around here. You look pretty tired out."

"Well, it's been quite a day, coming here with Miss Miller, being taken to Max's by Mr. Rutherford, being hauled away by Max

291

and brought here again, and then, when Jack came and Max had to escape, he threw me down and kicked me in the cracked ribs. And on top of all that, Mr. Rutherford's suicide. That is just too much to digest at one time."

"We'd better get you to a doctor."

"I'd rather go home."

He opened the door for me. "Oh, where can you be reached? We'll need you for further questioning, perhaps; certainly we'll want to know where to find you when it comes to testifying at the trial."

"Whose trial?"

"Max Baker's."

"You're awfully sure you'll get him, aren't you?" I gave him the address of the shop. In the big drawing room, I saw with relief that Rutherford's body had been removed. On the floor there was a chalked outline of his body as it had lain when it tumbled out of his chair, and on the magnificent carpet there was a horrible stain. Men were milling around, making sketches, talking to the maids and the chef. In the dining room, Miss Miller sat at the table, crying, dabbing her eyes, sniffling, answering questions in a distraught, disjointed manner that was manifestly irritating to the man who questioned her. It was a pity that genuine suffering should appear merely tiresome and somewhat ridiculous to an outsider, though I supposed that the police, like doctors and nurses, could not afford to become emotionally involved.

There was no sign of Forrest. Apparently he was undergoing questioning in another room.

Jack, who was standing at one of the long windows watching the police, studying the great room with more curiosity than admiration — I wondered what he would think of Max's apartment — came promptly to meet me. "I've been waiting for you. I'll take you home, Miss Bartlett."

"Thanks a lot, but that won't be necessary. I'm going straight down to the shop. My brother will be there."

"You aren't going alone. I'll call May, and then I'll take you wherever you are going. As long as that guy Max is on the loose, you aren't to be out by yourself."

I turned to the detective who had been questioning me. "Will you please give a message to Mr. Preston? Tell him I've gone down to my brother's antique shop." I gave him the address and telephone number.

And then Forrest came out of the small breakfast room, accompanied by a couple of men, his usually smooth hair rumpled as though he had been running his hand through it, his necktie loosened.

"Jennifer!"

"Mr. Logan is going to take me down to the shop."

"I'll take you," he said and gave Jack a curious look. I knew then that, like myself, he realized that Jack could have prevented the suicide. Like me, he was relieved that Jack had let Rutherford take his own way out.

The two men shook hands and Forrest promised to keep in touch. He smoothed his hair, straightened his tie, and shrugged into his overcoat.

"I'll be back," he told the police. "I might as well stay here until we've cleaned up all the details. And there are a whale of a lot of files to check, not only here but at the downtown office. Someone should get there at once to make sure no outsider can put his hands on the files. As soon as word of the suicide is out, his colleagues will be falling all over themselves trying to get rid of any incriminating information."

He took my arm and steered me out of the apartment. It was for the last time. I felt curiously deflated, let down, like an overindulged child after the excitement of Christmas morning.

Not until we were out of doors did I realize how many hours had passed since Rutherford had put a bullet through his head and the police had taken over. It was night. The buildings across Central Park were blazing with light. After the overheated apartment, the air on Fifth Avenue seemed clear and clean and sweet. I lifted my head and felt it cold and soothing on my face. As Forrest started to hail a taxi I said, "Please, I'd like to walk a little bit."

"With a sprained ankle and cracked ribs and after what you've been through today, I should think you'd be in no shape to walk."

"I need it. Walking helps me think."

"And what do you have to think about at this point?"

"Don't be so supercilious and superior," I snapped.

"You know something, Jennifer? Part of the time you have me standing on my head and liking it. But none of the time do I like shrews. What was that wonderful Elizabethan phrase: roaring girls. They are fun to read about but hell to live with."

"Well, you don't —" I broke off.

He did not attempt to make me finish the phrase. After a moment he said, "What do you have to think about?"

"Max. As long as Max is free, I'm not safe and Jimmy won't be safe — and very likely

Mrs. Rutherford. As for poor Rose Miller . . ."

"She asked for it." He was unsympathetic.

"I've been thinking and thinking, wondering what I would do if I were Max."

Forrest began to laugh. "Like the village idiot who found the missing horse by deciding where he would go if he were a horse?"

"Tell me a better way."

"He's painted himself into a corner," Forrest pointed out. "No money, a conspicuous outfit, a very conspicuous appearance."

"Just what I was thinking. But Max is no fool. And you act as though, locked out of his apartment, he has no place to go. A man like Max has someone to whom he can turn. He is bound to have. Someone who can provide him with at least a temporary shelter from the police, provide food and money, a change of clothes, even . . ."

"Well? Don't stop now."

"Even," I said slowly, "a change of appearance. You know what, Forrest? The police aren't going to run Max down by using that photograph. It won't be a guide by the time they show it."

"So what?"

"So I'm going to look for him."

"That is what you think," Forrest said grimly. "I can tell you right now, Jennifer, you aren't going anywhere but back to your brother's shop. And if he can't keep you out of trouble, then I'll take you on myself."

"Forrest —"

He shook his head. "You aren't going anywhere. I'll get a cab and take you home."

I clutched at his arm. "Forrest! Please! Please! If we could just use our heads, I know we could find Max. Think about it. There must be some sort of retreat he's had in the past, not far from where his apartment is. He wouldn't dare be unavailable for any length of time because he never knew when Rutherford would send for him. He was — at least I think he was — more interested in men than in women. Aren't there bars, places where he could encounter —"

"Sure, but if you think I am taking you to a place like that you are out of your mind."

"And where would I be safer?" I retorted.

He laughed at that. Then he shrugged. "Okay, you win. We'll try it."

Two bars failed to reveal Max. The third was, I thought, going to be another flop. And then I saw Max's unmistakable profile. I looked a second time. He was wearing a long blond wig that hung to his shoulders, a ruffled shirt, a pink jacket, and his eyelids were made up with a green eye shadow.

I clutched Forrest's arm and he followed

my eyes. "Max?" he said incredulously.

I nodded vigorously.

"Are you sure?"

"Positive."

We finished our drinks hastily and went out. I thought the proprietor was glad to see me go, though he had been courteous enough.

Forrest steered me up to the nearest traffic policeman, opened his billfold and spoke quietly and quickly. The policeman nodded.

"What do we do now?" I asked.

"We wait."

A few minutes later an unmarked car drew in to the curb and Forrest stepped forward. There was a hurried consultation and then Forrest, after a fierce whisper — "You stay here! Don't move!" — led them into the bar.

I don't know what I expected, as arrests on television are accompanied either by terrifying chases or by much gunfire, but in a few minutes the three men came out, accompanied by Max and a much younger man, hardly more than a boy, who was white-faced and terrified.

"Not Max!" he kept exclaiming. "Not Max!"

Forrest joined me. "Shall we go now?"

I was furious. "Damn it, you can't treat me like this! What happened?"

He laughed. "It's so easy to get a rise out of you that it's not even sporting. All right, one of the detectives tapped Max on the shoulder and said, 'Max Baker? I have a warrant for your arrest for kidnapping, extortion —' and before he could go on, Max, like the fool he is, drew his gun. They chopped it out of his hand, which is why you saw him handcuffed. Otherwise they'd have made a quiet, inconspicuous arrest. Oh, and they found a long green envelope in his pocket containing a bearer bond, a bunch of keys, and a woman's billfold. Think you could claim it?"

I was chagrined and he laughed again. "And that," he smiled down at me, "is that. You can stop thinking now."

"Good," I said. "Let's go home."

# 19

When I opened the door of the shop, I could hear voices from the apartment upstairs, several men and a woman. As I limped up the stairs Philip came running to meet me. "Jennifer! This is the best sight I've seen since you left here." He reached out to take me in his arms and saw Forrest behind me, supporting me the best he could. The brightness died out of his face. "I guess you must be Preston."

"And you are Hanning, who has been running a port of missing men."

They measured one another, giving the impression of strange dogs circling, and they did not attempt to shake hands.

Then Jimmy called, "That you, Jen?" And he came out to give me a crushing hug.

I cried out, "My ribs! My ribs! Be careful."

He held me back. "Sorry. Yeah, you do look a bit battered. When I get my hands on that guy —"

"It's all taken care of," Forrest assured him. "Max is under arrest and Rutherford shot himself three hours ago."

There was a choked cry and Mrs. Rutherford came to meet me.

"I'm sorry," I said. "I didn't mean it to be broken to you like this."

"Oh, the police told me about it at the airport and explained there was no further occasion for a divorce, but I didn't want to go home. I wanted to be with — my family," and she touched Jimmy's arm. "Were you there when it happened?"

I nodded. Somehow I could not dredge up all the easy platitudes: He didn't suffer. . . . Perhaps this was the best way. . . . I am so sorry. I wasn't sorry. I had been starved and stunned and horrified and sickened. But I wasn't sorry.

She relieved me of the necessity for any dishonesty on my part. "Thank God it is over," she told me simply. "I can't pretend about Paul any more. I have feared him for years and hated him for months. My dear, how much I owe you — you and Jimmy and dear Philip, who has been a guardian angel to us all."

Forrest stepped back. "I am leaving you in good hands."

I tugged at Jimmy's sleeve. He was being inexcusably rude. "Jimmy, this is Forrest Preston; Forrest, my brother."

"I know," Forrest said. "I saw the resemblance at once."

Jimmy nodded. "How are you, Preston?" A slap in the face would have been more friendly.

It was Mrs. Rutherford, again uncharacteristically taking the initiative, who said, "Don't go yet, Forrest. I'd like to have all the details now and then be able to forget about it."

She did not seem to observe that Jimmy failed to second her invitation. I saw my dear brother studying Forrest with a hostile expression on his face. But he couldn't, I thought, find anything to criticize in his appearance or his manners. After a faint, inquiring look at me, and seeing me nod, Forrest sat down. He must have felt that he had settled in a lion's den, the same generally cozy atmosphere, the same friendly attitude. I could cheerfully have slapped Jimmy.

At least he did bestir himself and remember that he was the host of this uncongenial party, and he poured sherry for us all, though I knew Forrest would have preferred Scotch or a martini at this hour. Exhausted as I was I began to wonder how long it was since I had eaten anything — breakfast, I thought.

I held the stage, telling them everything

that had happened from the time I had met Mrs. Rutherford at Tiffany's, when a photographer's attempt to take a picture of her buying a diamond bracelet for her dead daughter had provided me with the pretext I needed to meet her.

She merely nodded thoughtfully. "I'm glad you destroyed the film. A story like that would be hard to live down. I'd have had to spend the rest of my life assuring people that I am in my right mind."

I went on to Max's first kidnapping when I got off the Fifth Avenue bus, through his tying me up and my escape from the apartment, the jump from the fire escape, and my rescue by Tom O'Connor and Big Jack Logan.

Philip smiled. "But you'll always find men to come to your rescue, Jennifer." But there was no smile in his eyes.

"What I can't figure out," Jimmy said, "is why you were such a fool as to go back to Rutherford's apartment." He was disgusted. "You knew what the setup was. You knew what kind of rat Max was. You knew Rutherford was not to be trusted."

"Well, he had promised me my own terms. I thought there was a chance he would clear you of all those shameful allegations — saying that you had been responsible for Mary Ann's death and that you were a dishonest dealer and all that. And now he can't."

"I can clear Jimmy," Mrs. Rutherford said. "I will make any kind of statement that seems necessary. And I'll see that full restitution is made. And I'll tell everyone how proud I am to have Jimmy for a son-in-law." She got up. "I'm going to get to work right now. I'm going back to the apartment."

"That isn't necessary," Philip told her. "You are welcome to stay at my house as long as you like. It's going to seem empty with all my guests leaving at once." He did not look at me.

"I'll have to go back sooner or later," Mrs. Rutherford said, and I stared in amazement at this new woman, full of hope and confidence and making plans for herself. I began to understand how Pygmalion must have felt when his statue began to breathe. It was exhilarating but almost frightening at the same time, as though I had unleashed an unknown force for which I was, to some extent, responsible.

"There are a lot of things I want to pack." She smiled at me almost mischievously. "And those evening dresses. You must have them, my dear. Take them as a part of your trousseau." Before I could speak she went on, "I think I'll put the apartment up for sale."

"A three-story apartment on Fifth Avenue won't be easy to sell," Philip warned her.

"With rich Arabs and Japanese milling around, there will be plenty of potential buyers," she said with her new assurance. "And I'll get rid of that monstrous Long Island house. No one can keep up a house like that any more. I may turn it into a home for retired people on fixed incomes or a school for exceptional children. So much is being done to house the criminals, the girls who are taken off the street and return as through a revolving door, and the backward children who have a definite ceiling of achievement. Let's give the productive ones a break. Or" — with a sudden return to grim reality — "if Paul's money isn't all dishonest, I'd like to establish at least one medical school for aspiring young men who want to be doctors and don't have the opportunity to study. I'll buy a nice little apartment on Beekman Place and take along a couple of servants. I can hardly wait."

Jimmy reached out to silence the telephone. I could see his green eyes sparkling like a sunny sea, so I knew it was someone he liked. I wondered uneasily if my own eyes betrayed me so shamelessly. Then he said, "Yes, Jennifer is here after more hair-raising excitement. As you heard, she was kidnapped a second time. The newest development is that Max has been arrested and Rutherford put a bullet through his head. . . . Well, I can't say I blame you. . . . What's that? Oh, yes, I'll tell her."

He set down the phone. "Uncle Bert is leaving for London in the morning, now that you are out of durance vile. He said New York is too exciting for a quiet man. Oh, and he said to tell you, Jennifer, that if you have no other honeymoon plans he suggests his little hunting lodge. It's not uncomfortable, even by American standards, and there is some good fishing."

Philip got up, his smile a little forced. "What a pity that I don't fish!" He bent over and kissed me lightly on the cheek. "All the best, my dear; I want you to be happy." He took Mrs. Rutherford's arm. "I'll see you back to your apartment and make sure you are all right. We'd better stop somewhere and have dinner. Your stuff will be too disorganized tonight." He summoned up a grin for Jimmy. "You'll always find me at the old stand." They went down the stairs and the outside door of the shop closed.

"He's a hell of a good guy," Jimmy told me reproachfully.

"I know. The very best."

"It's a wonder to me that you can look him in the face. He's a better man than you deserve, Jen. If you had seen the way he came barging down to the hospital and looked after me. And the way he coped with Mrs. Rutherford, with men watching his house twenty-four hours a day and trailing him wherever he went. And took the whole thing as though it were good fun. And then," Jimmy went on bitterly, "Uncle Bert assumes you are going to marry Preston, whom you haven't known a week."

"What right has he —" I could feel the color rising in my cheeks, and I knew that Forrest was watching me.

"Well, aren't you?" Jimmy asked in astonishment. "I thought that was your reason for giving Philip the old heave-ho."

I could have strangled Jimmy, and an hour before I had been heartbroken at not clearing him. Right now I could cheerfully have ground his face in some gravel. "Well — I don't know — and he doesn't like roaring girls — and . . ."

Forrest laughed. "At least a man ought to be allowed to do his own courting."

There is a limit to everything. "Well, why

don't you?" I suggested.

"What about — a little — maidenly — reticence?" he asked between kisses.

I pulled away from him, trying to get my breath.

"Come back here."

I went.

"Well now," Jimmy said, producing the first practical suggestion of his life, "isn't it time for us all to go out to dinner?"

We hope you have enjoyed this Large Print book. Other Thorndike Press or Chivers Press Large Print books are available at your library or directly from the publishers.

For more information about current and upcoming titles, please call or write, without obligation, to:

Thorndike Press
P.O. Box 159
Thorndike, Maine 04986 USA
Tel. (800) 257-5157

OR

Chivers Press Limited
Windsor Bridge Road
Bath BA2 3AX
England
Tel. (0225) 335336

All our Large Print titles are designed for easy reading, and all our books are made to last.